TANGLEWOOD

Andrea Grace was an ambitious singer and she knew that the enigmatic band-leader Gabriel Fox was just the man to help her become a star. Nothing — not even his arrogance and cruel dominance — would stand in her way, she vowed. Even the unexpected arrival of love, powerful and bitter-sweet as it was, took second place to Andrea's first love, the theatre. Only a terrible tragedy proved it to be the other way around . . .

*Books by Barbara Grim
in the Linford Romance Library:*

THE COTTAGE OF CONTENT

BARBARA GRIM

TANGLEWOOD

Complete and Unabridged

LINFORD
Leicester

First published in Great Britain in 1992 by
Robert Hale Limited
London

First Linford Edition
published 2000
by arrangement with
Robert Hale Limited
London

British Library CIP Data

Grim, Barbara, *1939* –
Tanglewood.—Large print ed.—
Linford romance library
1. Love stories
2. Large type books
I. Title
823.9′14 [F]

ISBN 0–7089–5761–7

Published by
F. A. Thorpe (Publishing)
Anstey, Leicestershire
Set by Words & Graphics Ltd.
Anstey, Leicestershire
Printed and bound in Great Britain by
T. J. International Ltd., Padstow, Cornwall

This book is printed on acid-free paper

To Gemma

1

Andrea sat in front of the mirror, perfectly still, with her head tilted. She heard a click as the door closed, abruptly cutting off the silvery-voiced saxophone. She was alone, then. Just she and her thoughts cocooned in velvet walls and exotic scents.

Only the faint thud of drums penetrated this womb-like boudoir, or was it her heart, she wondered? Stop acting like a fool Andrea — pull yourself together. It was unexpected — OK, a shock — but no need to go to pieces like this. Fingernails dug into her sticky palms and she could have wept at the inner turmoil that had so suddenly shattered her peaceful existence.

Comb and scent — ordinary, every-day things — would be in the beaded bag Jane would have placed directly in front of her. Her fingers glided over the

1

cool slippery surface of the dressing-table. Glass, she supposed, and wondered if lights glowed in a circle around the mirror. Her knee touched drapes and she heard quite clearly the faint rustle of crisp frills.

The white stick rested there. Within reach.

Ignoring the comb she ran fingers through her hair, as she often did. Silken strands brushed her cheeks, tangling with her lashes. She lifted her hair high, then let it fall, enjoying its fresh lemon scent — like a breath of country air in the cloying atmosphere of the ladies' room. Surely with hair smelling so sweet she must be pretty!

What did she look like to him now? Her hands went to her high-boned cheeks exploring their fullness; she traced the heart shape right down to the point of her chin. What had he seen this evening when they had met for the first time in five years?

He had recognized her immediately, although she no longer had the boyish haircut and blonde streaks. Long, straight and dead brown was how Jane, in her forthright Aussie manner, described Andrea's hair. How dull! She could, she supposed, go to the hairdresser tomorrow and change the colour; perhaps have streaks again. But what was the use? She wouldn't see him again after tonight, so what difference will tomorrow make?

'What Difference Will Tomorrow Make?' She caught her breath. That had been the title of one of her songs. Haunting, sad, different from the rock and roll numbers she usually sang. How did it go? She started to hum. 'What difference will tomorrow make, now my lover has gone? Tomorrow will make no difference at all . . . Just another day without the parting, another yesterday without love.'

Yesterday without love . . .

The sense of unreality persisted. Had it really happened? Was it a dream? She went over the events of the past hour . . .

★　★　★

The speeches over — the Company
Chairman leaving the stage and returning to the top table — polite applause
breaking into a buzz of chatter and
laughter — the scent of coffee, cigar
smoke, mint and brandy.

Startled by the sudden blast of
trumpets, Andrea had jumped, unaware
that their table was so close to the
stage. As clarinets, trombones and
piano intertwined she gave up all
attempts to converse, listening intently
instead as a saxophone played with the
emotions of the dancers; she sensed the
carousel of movement by a fragrant
breeze from their bodies — the touch of
their skirts as they whirled past.

'Dance Andrea?'

'Sure.' She delved into the crush of
bodies, and despite her limp gave
herself up to the rhythm of a slow
foxtrot, until the music stopped and
someone announced the interval.

Bony fingers gripped her wrist,

guiding her into the chair.

'How'd it go Andrea?'

'Thanks Jane. Got stabbed by a stiletto heel. How about you?'

'Who wants to dance with this lot?' came the brusque reply. 'There's no one interesting enough to describe to you even, except the bloke on the stage.'

Andrea bent down to rub her ankle. 'Who?'

'The bandleader. In that suit he looks like an overstuffed penguin. More like an outdoor type. Tall — legs like tree trunks — narrow waist going up to wide shoulders.'

Andrea chuckled. 'Which animal is he?'

'A Tasmanian Devil.'

'A what?'

'Like a bear, but smaller, with a big dark head, white chest and an irritable look. Oh!'

Andrea felt warm breath on her face as Jane hissed in her ear, 'He's coming this way.'

Instinctively Andrea sat up and turned her head.

Her fingers were crushed in a large damp palm and from way above came a voice she had never expected to hear again. 'Andy! I don't believe it.'

Her heart jerked and she sat in stunned silence, until, conscious of her gaping mouth she took a deep breath and cleared her throat. 'Gabby?'

Who else had a voice like milk chocolate and words like bullets? She had once told him he sounded like a bar of chocolate hazel nut.

But he was still holding her hand . . . he was speaking. 'Going to give us a song Andy?'

She licked dry lips and tried to tug her hand from his grasp. 'I can't . . . I don't sing now.'

'With a voice like yours . . . ?' He sounded shocked, releasing her hand with a suddenness that left her floundering; yet she could still sense the nearness of his powerful body and smell the sandalwood aftershave and soap he had always used.

'I'm sure your friends would love to hear you sing,' he commanded. 'Come on.'

With her acute sensitivity she felt vibrations of curiosity and shock surging around her, even before they called out.

'Please.'

'Go on Andrea.'

But she shook her head, conscious that those close to her hung on to every word the bandleader was saying to their telephonist.

They don't know my heart and stomach are doing a flip, she thought, swallowing hard. 'No, Gabby, it's been too long, not since . . .'

She heard a heavy, pained sigh and imagined the sombre look he would be wearing; remembering how, when thwarted, a certain expression would sweep across his swarthy features, making him appear surly. Yet recalling too, the contrast when he smiled and deep ravines each side of his mouth ran up to meet the crinkles around his eyes, changing a face that was really unexceptional into one of devastating and disturbing charm.

Flatly, she added, 'Besides, it's impossible for me to go on stage again. Just impossible.'

There was a hurt silence, until her shadows suddenly became a lighter shade of dark and she guessed the main lights had gone on.

'Andy . . . my God!'

He's seen the white stick, she thought, because the words seemed to tangle in his throat. And because he pressed her shoulder and left without saying goodbye.

Surrounded by a babel of questions she attempted a shaky smile, shook her head and raised a warning hand, glad that the disc jockey employed to fill the interval gap spun records with loud enthusiasm. Enough to make conversation impossible and to allow her to sort through painfully disturbed feelings.

Her effort to re-engage herself with

the person she had been at the start of the evening failed miserably. Having the past placed before her, when she had cut herself off so completely, gave her the eerie sensation of stepping out of time.

The returning band started with a rousing quickstep which she couldn't do. But her heart beat to the rhythm. Her foot tapped. Later the mood changed, and piano notes traced the outline of a wistful love song, called, she remembered so well, 'Melancholy Out Of A Song'.

Gabriel took the mike. So he has no singer now, she thought wistfully. A mediocre singer, nevertheless his voice blended with the atmosphere, seducing couples on to the floor. He strolled to the edge of the stage and down the steps. Avoiding the swaying dancers and trailing the wire, he saw her in the corner, a little mouse with a sheet of brown hair the same rich shade as her velvet dress, her chin tilted so that he fancied she beckoned . . .

At that moment music was her only reality. Evocative chords spun her emotions until she could no longer deny the summons. She stood — swaying like a cobra to the rhythm. Easily she slipped into a duet with his hand covering hers over the mike, voices mingling as always. Expertly she weaved, ebbed and flowed around his uncertain bass, with that extraordinary wide range endowed upon her by nature.

Thus five years disappeared as if they had never been.

Clapping and cheering broke out all around as the last notes died away, and Andrea returned to the present, disorientated and confused.

His lips brushed her ear. 'Beautiful. See you later.' Then he was gone, leaving a trail of sandalwood in the darkness. She wanted to cry out, scream like a baby, as she strove for the first time in years to see. Instead she stood like a statue while friends crowded around — congratulating, shaking her hand, patting her on the back. And afterwards she supposed that she had smiled and said all the right things . . . until she had asked Jane to take her away . . .

★   ★   ★

She reached out towards the mirror, searching for electric bulbs. There were none, of course, they shone only in her memory, the lights around the mirror. Like planets circling the sun, they were all she retained from her seeing years. The rest she had hidden away after the accident, or mislaid in pain and darkness, concentrating all her efforts on the fight to accept her blindness.

Tonight, then, had really happened — it was no dream. And no matter how hard she tried to stop them, her thoughts insisted upon returning to the early days, before the accident, and she trembled with emotion as memories crept out of the darkness, into the light . . .

2

Light bulbs glared into the flushed young face. Andrea snatched a brush from the jumble of pots, bottles and boxes on the dressing-table and traced dark shader down the lower part of her round cheeks. Brown shadow on her lids matched her eyes and dark pencil enhanced their almond shape. Pouting into the mirror she slicked on pale lipstick because there was no reason to draw attention to a mouth which was in her opinion too small.

There was a sudden rap on the door. 'Ten minutes Miss Grace.'

Her hand jerked, sending a bottle crashing down. 'Damn!' She flicked it upright and tugged the linen band from her head. Then all she had to do was to tease her fringe into shape and smooth her hair into the nape of her neck, turning this way and that way to enjoy the glint of highlights. Then, satisfied, she tore off her wrapper. With shaking hands she smoothed the lurex mini-skirted dress, which was already wrinkle free, and checked that the knee-length white boots were zipped up.

She was ready to step out into the chilly corridor with its peeling beige paint, and that smell! After just two years she felt as if she had moved in it all her life. The smell of greasepaint, gin and fear.

From beyond heavy curtains came the twang and beat of guitar and drums — a burst of applause. Just in time she stood back as four boys running from the stage almost cannoned into her, blinded as they were by excitement and perspiration running down their faces.

Her heart thumped. This was it. Her first solo. No going back. There was an inner coldness, churning stomach, a dry mouth, tight throat — and then, the opening bars of her music. With nowhere else to go, she went forward, into the glare, her body as rigid as the mike. What would she do without that cold skinny body to hang on to? Unprofessional, they said, to hug the mike.

Her dry lips parted . . .

The notes came out loud and clear, surely from another throat. Perhaps that man down there waving his baton; how it irritated her when he mouthed the words as she sang. Yet she gained comfort from staring at him. Because she mustn't look beyond him to the rows of white upturned staring blobs. It was like being afraid of heights and knowing you mustn't look down.

Her hands on the mike were clammy, and surely her mascara must be running . . .

Then she was aware of her own voice; pleased when she hit the high notes — breathing into the low notes — working at it — starting to enjoy the sound she made. Little by little a sensation of pure joy rose until her chest threatened to burst with emotion.

Always there came a point when she

breathed waves of powdery perfume from the audience. Feeling their pleasure match her own, she loosened up, dancing to her song. Clutching the hand mike she wriggled and jived to the beat until she heard the audience clapping with her.

Then she threw back her head and sang her heart out.

And only then was she able to look down at them. Andrea paused at the stage door. Ostensibly to tug her jacket more securely around her shoulders against the wind and rain, but really to stand in the hollow. Her own little ritual, with a hint of superstition.

In common with many theatres, this gracious building was crumbling and worn in parts. Dressing-rooms were shabby, lacking modern conveniences; the plumbing was noisy and unreliable, and the stage doorstep depressed by a century of use.

When years before, Andrea had been taken for the first time to a theatre, she had, with childish curiosity, searched for the stage door. She had placed her feet in the worn saucer-shaped step, moved to tears thinking of the stars who had passed that way. One day, she vowed, I will tread in their footsteps.

Her father, she remembered, had been impatient with her dream, disappointed that the girl who until then had seemed as level-headed as himself should reveal such a fanciful side to her nature. He never stopped reminding her that he had looked forward to her following him into the police force.

Someone prodded her in the back. 'Go on Andrea. There's the car.'

Lowering her head she ran through the rain and threw herself into the corner of the limousine with her friends clambering in behind her. Doors slammed, muffling the street noises. Shiny rainbow colours slipped past the window — umbrellas, coats, scarves — she imagined one's expensive hair-do blowing in the wind, or a new outfit splashed with mud, comparing it to the blissful comfort of the leather-smelling car.

Funny how she had to search for enjoyment lately, forcing comparisons with the past in order to emphasize how lucky she now was. But when I get to a West End theatre, she thought fiercely, I'll be over the moon.

'What's it like going solo luv?' asked Gerry.

She turned from the rain spattered window. 'Terrifying.'

'You were great Andy,' grinned Sean.

Spike put on a scowl. 'Shut up. She won't want to sing with us if you make her too big-headed.'

The car rocked as the boys, light-hearted with relief after the strain of performing, indulged in horseplay.

Andrea began to relax too. 'Stop it, Jimmy,' she giggled, dragging him from the window where he was pulling faces at astonished passers-by. In twenty minutes they reached the brightly lit West End, where the car, too big for the narrow back streets, proceeded slowly towards the nightclub. Spilling out of the car, they swooped beneath the nose of a doorman into the wide pink mouth that panted with noise and movement.

Andrea prickled with anticipation. Coming off stage created a void. What could follow it? Certainly not her parents' drab sitting-room in a dark back street; she shuddered, welcoming the thud of bass.

An arm slipped around her waist. 'Wine?' asked a voice in her ear.

She turned and almost collided with a stubbled chin. 'Yes please Spike.' She watched him push through a maze of bodies and chattering mouths.

'Sorry. I didn't hear you.' She bent her head towards Gerry.

His hot breath fanned her cheek. 'I said what time are you going?'

She wrinkled her nose. 'Midnight. Like Cinderella.'

He gave her a sly look. 'We're going upstairs for a game on the tables at 11.30.'

'Then I might not ring for the cab

until later,' she smiled. 'I'm open to new experiences.'

'Then stay at our place in Clapham?' Jimmy winked. 'If you enjoy new experiences . . . '

'I'd like to, Jimmy,' she began. What stops me, she wondered? She hated going home after the performance; clubs such as these were a necessary bridge between the theatre and the sleeping Kentish country town. If only her father wouldn't sit up for her, making it an obligation, somehow. Although more and more often lately, unable to tear herself away, she had found him asleep.

A glass was thrust into her hand and she gulped down the wine. It was easier after that to put her indecision to one side and enjoy being buffeted by words and waves of spirit until her head was swimming.

There was a voice — deep and resonant — heard above the hubbub — somewhere behind her. 'So this is the famous Sullen Andy.'

Turning, she looked up, and up. Past a square chin, full lips parted in a crooked half smile, an important nose to ice blue, hostile eyes.

She felt her cheeks redden. 'I beg your pardon.'

His reply was lost in bursts of laughter and he suddenly grasped her elbow and pulled her to one side. Taken by surprise, she moved with him. He's going to buy me a drink at the bar, she thought, until she found herself heading for the door.

At once, she tried to pull her arm from his hard fingers. 'Just a minute. I was talking to my friends . . . '

But his grip tightened and suddenly she was in the foyer and the slowly closing doors were cutting off the noise. Only their footsteps rang on the floor.

'Get your coat,' he ordered. 'I want to go somewhere where we can talk.'

She stopped dead. 'Not on your life. I don't know you.'

He received his coat from the girl behind the desk. 'And good girls don't go out with strange men.' He turned to her with a mocking smile.

'Here you are miss.'

Andrea glared at the flustered girl and grabbed the jacket, holding it in front of her.

Heaving an exaggerated sigh, he reached into the pocket of his dinner jacket and brought out a card.

She turned her head away. Why should she care who this odious man is? Then overcome by curiosity she snatched it from his fingers, holding it out as if it burned.

'Well, Mr Gabriel Fox, Bandleader. What do you want with me?'

'I told you. I want to talk to you. Business.'

'Why the bad manners?' she sneered. 'Why not ask politely?'

His dark brows rose with the air of a man who was unused to being talked back to, especially by a young girl. 'I tried, but you didn't hear me in that scrum — I asked to speak to you alone.'

'You don't even know me. What in

the hell do you want to talk about?'

'Your life.'

'What,' she asked icily, 'has it to do with you?'

He waved an arm towards the pink padded doors. 'You're destroying it, that's what. And your career. Booze, late nights, wrong songs . . . '

'Oh no,' Andrea allowed herself a tight smile. 'You have the wrong girl Mr-er . . . Fox. You should have been at the theatre tonight and seen my first solo.'

'I was,' he said flatly. 'And I did.'

Her chin lifted. 'Well then?' The curious faces of the cloakroom girl and a man in a dress suit turned towards them.

She lowered her voice. 'My fans . . . '

'Oh dear,' he laughed, and she gasped, engulfed in flames of hatred for this stranger, who must surely be a madman. Turning away, she shook her head, almost bowled over by savage fangs of temper which left her trembling, and her throat aching with the effort of holding back angry tears.

She felt his grasp on her elbow and twisted to glare up into his face, throwing back her head and speaking through gritted teeth. 'This is a nightmare. There I was, just minutes ago, enjoying myself with my friends, without a care in the world, and now,' — she pulled away from him, waving her arms in the air — 'I'm being insulted by a stranger with a high-class accent.'

He ignored her outburst. 'Fans live in a dream world. One day they awake. When they do they'll chuck you out. And that day, believe me, isn't far away. You'll be finished before you've started.'

His voice was deep and smooth, his words brutal, and she shook her head dumbly, unable any longer to prevent tears seeping into her eyes.

His voice roughened, almost showing emotion. 'You don't have to wait for that day. Put that glorious voice where it belongs. In front of people who thrill to a quality voice, not a beat.'

Coming no higher than his shoulder she stood her ground, matching glare for glare; his eyes smouldered with intensity — hers swam with tears.

She would have the last word, she vowed, feeling the heat in her cheeks. And it would be as venomous and dismissive as she could make it.

Startled, she saw his expression turn to amused affection. Creases scuttled across his face and lines swept upwards to meet crinkles each side of his eyes; the whole of his face disintegrated and reassembled into sweetness so instantly she almost staggered at the impact and somehow mislaid the caustic sentences that were forming in her mind.

His eyes darkened and he turned away, striding towards the ornate double doors. 'Cab please,' he called to the doorman, sliding his hand into his pocket.

'Yes sir.' The doorman went out into the dark slippery street.

Gabriel Fox no longer held her. But she meekly followed.

3

She trailed after Gabriel's broad back to an alcove where the waiter flicked away imaginary specks and bowed them to their red plush seats. Eating was serious business, she noted; music and conversation harmonized perfectly, neither intruding upon the other. Smells also mingled well — rich and creamy, succulent and sharp, savoury and sweet — predominantly of expensive perfume and coffee.

'Mm. Different.'

His mouth curled. 'From the dives you're used to, I expect it is.'

'I'm quite happy as I am thank you,' she snapped.

'Are you? Then why the sullen face all the time?'

She shrugged. 'You know what reporters are . . . '

He picked up the menu. 'Let's get

25

this sorted out, then we'll talk.'

Once again she prickled with resentment at his autocratic manner, but pressed her lips together and bent over the menu.

'Now,' he said in his clipped voice as the waiter disappeared with their order, 'I've been wanting to meet you for some time — you're an elusive little lady. Once you come off stage you disappear with those friends of yours. Probably into deepest Soho.'

'It's none of your business,' she warned. 'What do you want with me anyway?'

'I have gut reactions when I meet new talent.'

She was speechless. Idly she twirled the stem of the glass between her fingers, acting out her disinterest in what this odious man was saying.

'Do you remember when you reached the finals in the television talent show?' he demanded.

'How could I forget? Up until then I'd only sung in pubs and clubs.'

He nodded. 'Not doing much better now, are you? Still bottom of the bill. Do you remember the judges?'

'There were three,' she said sulkily. 'Two women and . . . ' Her voice trailed away. 'And you.'

He chuckled. 'You've a short memory.'

'It was three years ago,' she retorted. 'And I was so nervous. It was all a blur really.'

Brass wall lights set his eyes glowing. 'I've been tied up over the last two years . . . ' he hesitated, 'with contracts, and personal problems; I've just finished a tour of Germany. But I hoped — indeed intended — to meet you again. Your unusual voice — its depth, its variation — fascinated me. Such a mature voice for one so young . . . '

She studied this strange man. Brutal, dominant, insensitive, rude — sympathetic and flattering, saturnine yet cheerful — she had been in the company of half a dozen men in the last hour, instead of merely one.

How could I have gone with him so easily? How can he meddle with my emotions the way he does? I'm alternately angry, insulted, deflated — and yet, curious too . . .

His black brows were raised. 'I was asking who your agent is.'

She tossed her head. 'We manage ourselves.'

He grunted and raised his glass. 'That's what I hoped.' A contented smile tugged at the corners of his mouth before he drank.

The waiter unloaded plates from the trolley and slid away, leaving them with their glances circling like wild animals across steaming bowls of soup.

'Some of the things I've heard about you Andrea . . . ' He shook his head slowly from side to side with his mouth pursed. 'You'll never make it with that group.'

She glared at him. 'I don't know what you mean, we're becoming more successful all the time.'

He gave a sarcastic laugh. 'Success

and stardom are understood — talent is open to interpretation.' He leaned forward, his face set in serious lines. 'You're too good for them. They wallow in an atmosphere of sex, violence and expensive cheap thrills. One is unshaven, another unkempt, and as for the one who puckers his lips, thrusts out a bony bum, cavorts and minces around the stage, well . . . words fail me.'

'Good,' she replied stonily.

As if she hadn't spoken, he went on, 'And then there's the drinking. Look, darling, in my time I've seen a band's drummer being carried to the drum stool; I've seen mikes knocked over; I've seen a comic trying to argue with the front row audience, and one vocalist threw booze over them. A singer I won't name once threw a mike stand and nearly took a roadie's head off!' Gabriel took a deep breath. 'Audiences deserve better than that, don't you think?'

Andrea sliced the delicious-looking lemon sole, chewed and found it tasted of cardboard. Beneath her lashes she watched Gabriel neatly cut his steak and help himself to vegetables. For a while there was silence.

When their dinner plates had been whisked away, desserts chosen, coffee ordered, he lit a cigar. 'Rock thinks it's a hallowed form of entertainment way beyond criticism. It isn't. One day the audience might prefer to spend their well-earned pounds on something else.'

She gulped down the last of her wine. 'You didn't bring me here just to preach a sermon, Mr Fox, or to save my soul. So what exactly is this leading up to?'

A look of surprise flashed across his face. 'I want you in my band as my lead singer. In return, I'll make you a star.'

She felt a wave of triumph. 'Do you really think I'm that naïve . . . ?'

His eyes glowed with amusement. 'Don't flatter yourself, Sullen Andy. I'm a good ten years older than you are, and, trite as it may sound, I really do only have a paternal interest.' He paused. 'The fact is . . . I know what I

30

want. You, as a star. Not your body.' He frowned. 'The world's full of glamorous bodies and faces. You have neither.'

The lemon sorbet stuck in her throat but she forced herself to carry on eating, keeping her eyes fixed on the silver bowl.

'I believe Andrea, that the public is in the mood for something different. The girl next door — plain and ordinary — just like them.' His voice gained momentum — his cheese and biscuits lay untouched. 'You won't sing in dance halls forever, just for experience. Eventually, under my management, you'll go solo. I see you on stage — no effects — just you in the spotlight, plain dress, unjewelled. No gimmick, just voice. Will you do it?'

It should have been one of the most wondrous moments of her life. Yet Andrea sat there afraid of the wetness in her eyes.

The waiter placed a cup before her and poured from a silver pot. It was steam from the coffee, she decided.

★ ★ ★

'For God's sake Andrea, stop jumping about.'

Trumpets, trombones and saxophone wailed to a stop. From her position in the centre of the hall Andrea kept her eyes on the men who were making a great fuss of sorting out sheet music.

'And please, *please* try to sing straight; no screams or whoops.' Gabriel tapped his baton against the piano.

'It's habit Gabriel. I . . . '

'Then snap out of it.' He raised his arms.

Biting her lip she turned her back on him, facing dingy cream walls and windows near the ceiling.

I'll give up, she fumed. It's hopeless trying to work with someone so obnoxious.

Thrusting her thumbs in the pocket of her jeans she took a deep breath and swaggered towards the door, watching Gabriel from the corner of her eye.

He shrugged, raised his arms higher

and the trombones began to play the introductory notes. Weaving into the pattern came piano and saxophone, until he dropped his arm to signal a pause. 'I want a cliff-hanging, vocal introduction here.'

Andrea turned.

The tomboy had gone. In her place stood a woman, poised and clothed in dignity, with her head held high. From this regal stranger came the familiar voice, soaring high up the scale, teetering there, fading, swooping down to earth and settling, warm and low. Yet it too was clothed in new depth, throbbing and echoing around the hall. Anyone looking at Gabriel would have seen him freeze and swallow. But no one saw. They all watched the girl with the woman's voice, who remained motionless, and simply sang.

The last notes faded away. In a dreamy state, only half aware at first of the burst of clapping, it wasn't until Gabriel put down his baton that she came to life. Unable to stop her face from splitting into a grin, she waved to the applauding chorus girls. When she saw him striding towards her, she turned expectantly, with her heart thumping, to face him . . .

'That's more like it Andrea, about time too. Wasn't too difficult to stand still, was it? But you aren't royalty you know.'

Colour swamped her face. Her arm fell to her side, hand clenched into a ball. When he went to stride past her she caught his shirt sleeve and threw back her head to stare up into a face that was twisted with impatience.

'Look,' she said between clenched teeth, 'I've taken a lot of stick from you in the last week.' When he went to speak she overrode him. 'Only *because*,' she sneered, 'I must admit you do know what you're talking about as far as the performance is concerned. And I want to learn. But when I stop singing,' her voice rose, '*don't* tell me how to behave. OK?'

Impaled by his eyes, and shaking with

fear, she refused to look away.

A crash shattered the silence.

The trombonist made a grab for his toppling music stand, missed and bent to retrieve the scattered sheet music. When he stood up they had turned away from each other and were stalking in opposite directions.

★ ★ ★

Andrea pushed her way through the chattering girls to reach the makeshift dressing-table. When she sat down someone placed a steaming plastic cup before her.

'Thanks Jill.' Andrea sipped the tea and looked up gratefully at the tall dancer. 'Every morning,' she addressed their reflections in the mirror, 'when I awake, I say to myself, 'today I will not row with Gabriel'.'

Jill's eyes in the mirror held a glow of sympathy. 'He can be a bad-tempered pig and a right old bully.'

Andrea nodded, mopping her face.

'I've been brought up to look after myself; I don't have to allow people, whether bullies or elders, to walk all over me. He fits both categories. I could hit him.'

She ran pink lipstick over her mouth and blotted it with a tissue.

The other girl laughed. 'Coming for a meal?'

Andrea shook her head. 'I've promised to visit the parents. I haven't been for ages and tonight it seems they have important news to impart.'

'Do they live far?'

'Only an hour away now I have the car.'

Jill tossed her cup into the bin and struggled into her coat. 'You're lucky. I left my mum and dad in Yorkshire. See you tomorrow chuck. Bye.'

★ ★ ★

'That's what we wanted to tell you Andrea.'

She studied her father's florid face,

noting his wary eyes and strained smile. 'Australia?' She shook her head in disbelief.

Her mother glanced at her husband and back to Andrea. 'We haven't seen you for months, dear.'

'Mum, I've been on the road, from ballroom to ballroom. Bournemouth, Blackpool, the Isle of Wight . . . '

'I know dear, we got your cards. I wasn't . . . '

Andrea felt her cheeks grow hot. 'I haven't spent more than a dozen nights in my own flat until this week.'

Her father's voice was sharp. 'We didn't want you to take this . . . ' he hesitated, 'this job with that Gabriel chap in the first place.'

'That was my own decision to make,' she flashed.

'And Australia,' he said heavily, 'was ours.'

'You're right Dad. But now we're in the theatre. Only a small one, but it's a start. No more ballrooms; home every night. Gabriel's tired of ballrooms too.'

Her parents exchanged glances. 'Come with us dear.'

'How can I Mum, I'm just getting started?' She hated the whine in her voice, but it seemed as if they were deliberately trying not to understand her point of view.

'Father's always wanted to join his brother in Australia. We both have,' her mother added quickly. 'Now he's retired from the police . . . '

'It's now or never,' he interrupted. 'You're not yet nineteen. Your uncle would give you a job in his office and I'd prefer you to come with us and settle down rather than roam about with Gabriel Fox.' His lip curled.

'You've always had something against him Dad. Why?'

'I should think so. He took my only daughter away from me didn't he?'

'That's not true Dad. I was in the theatre before I met him.'

He jerked his hand in the air. 'You went around with that pop group. It was just a hobby. You'd soon have forgotten the stage and found a proper job.'

'Never,' she spat. 'I love the theatre.'

'You've changed Andrea,' he said gruffly, 'since you've known him. Apart from the new car and your own flat, you've changed in yourself.'

She raised her eyes to the ceiling.

'You left the boys without a qualm.' He shook his head. 'You've changed.'

'For the better,' she retorted. 'With Gabriel I'll get on. He knows about show business — he has contacts.'

He sat forward, resting a hand on each knee. 'You have a crush on him haven't you?' His bulbous eyes were wide and anxious; his greying moustache quivered.

'Dad, you just don't understand. You haven't heard anything I've said.' Her voice broke. 'You're always so stubborn. You know best, and you won't listen to any other point of view.'

'I know people, Andrea. It's my job. And I tell you he's no good.'

She shook her head numbly, as he

went on. 'He has secrets that man. You can see it in his eyes. Secrets.'

With all the scorn she could muster, she retaliated. 'You're jealous Dad. Jealous.'

His mouth twisted. 'He'll betray you Andrea.'

He looked at her steadily, sure of himself, the man she had admired and tried, as a child, to emulate. Borrowing from him such characteristics as his self-control, his toughness, his strength she had turned from the mother she physically resembled because she saw how the woman moulded herself around the man, with an obsessive love. Andrea had no intention of subjugating herself to any man and travelling through life second class.

She saw her mother now, thin and jittery, perched on the edge of the chair; like a mouse, with her round cheeks and pointed nose, she had a habit of tilting her chin in the air as if sniffing for danger; her baby-like mouth constantly twitched and she nervously pulled at her drab hair.

Her father's voice broke into her thoughts. 'Come with us Andrea luv.'

Her throat ached. 'No Dad. No. I can't.'

The stubbornness in his mouth so matched her own; they both knew there was nothing more to say. But with the self-centredness of a child she knew that the thought of emptiness at the end of the road brought a feeling very much like panic.

Nevertheless, when the car tore across the Medway Bridge and the blackened hills of Kent closed behind her like gates, what circled around and around in her head was her father's words.

'He has secrets.'

4

The spotlight caught her at centre stage, momentarily blinding her to anything but a smoky path to the roof.

She was grasping the thin body of the mike, feeling her way shakily with the first few bars of the song. Like a candle in the slinky white off one shoulder dress and long white gloves, she burned with fright.

There was the dreaded longing to escape, to be anywhere but where she was. People in the audience coughed, cleared their throats, rustled programmes.

At her feet, Gabriel raised the baton higher. That first high note. Breathe, she told herself. Stand tall.

She threw back her head, releasing the high note in a sudden spurt. Then remembered nothing more except the enjoyment of singing to the warm mass of people she now held in her arms. Her voice went out to them, and their hearts bounded to meet her. She touched every person out there, probed their senses, invaded their dreams and memories, knowing they would go where she led and she could squeeze every emotion from them.

Towards the end of the song her voice rose — and dropped suddenly, to a whisper. She turned then, and walked away, leaving them up high. Wanting more. Where Gabriel expected them to be.

In the wings she tolerated hugs and kisses as people crowded around. Longingly, she looked back at the curtains hiding the stage until arms propelled her through them and she heard it again. The applause. Then she walked out on to that fearful space, afraid no longer.

Her face split into a grin as she raised her arms and stood alone before them. Those in the front rows were standing; she saw their faces. The mass became individuals, strangers who loved her. Excitement pumped her full of a sickness that threatened to rise to her throat.

'Encore! Encore!'

She caught Gabriel's eyes and he shook his head. With a last wave she dragged her steps from the stage.

Because there was nowhere else to go.

★ ★ ★

Andrea shivered, hearing the echo of applause. What's wrong with me? She sat at the dressing-table with the lights around the mirror glowing on to her anxious face and troubled eyes.

There was a rap on the door. Before she could call out it was flung open to reveal Gabriel and the boys of the band. Gabriel's long legs carried him across the room in an instant. Standing behind the chair with his hands lightly resting on her shoulders, he studied her reflection. 'Well done, darling.'

He pressed her shoulders gently, his thumbs lightly massaging the muscles at the base of her neck. Her heart somersaulted and the blood surged in her veins until she was warm once more.

Champagne splashed into her glass. 'Thanks Ben.' She grinned at the drummer.

'You were marvellous.'

'Thanks again.'

She prickled with excitement as the voices grew louder and more exuberant.

'Wasn't she good?'

'Wonderful.'

'A winner for you Gabriel.'

'Where's the party?'

'At the Gatsby I think.'

Gabriel pulled up a chair, sat down beside her and leaned forward. 'All right now darling?'

'Fine thanks.'

'Bit shaky were you just now?'

She nodded, smiling into his eyes.

'Reaction pet. You suffer badly from nerves and, let's face it, I gave you a

45

hard rehearsal.' His mouth twisted into a rueful grin.

There was that boyish charm she had seen so briefly and wondered if she had imagined. Could he be apologizing? It certainly seemed so?

He passed her a box of tissues. 'Get that stuff off Andy. We're going to a party.'

*   *   *

The restaurant was small and discreet, with dark plum walls and brass wall lamps. Lighted alcoves held marble statues and around the foyer wall hung signed photographs of famous show business patrons.

Soon the crowd, released from tension, set the place glowing, even the waiters joined them in a lusty sing song around the piano after the other customers had gone.

Just when she was fizzing with excitement and energy, her friends started to drift away.

'Don't go already,' she complained.

'We've a matinée tomorrow afternoon duckie,' Ben reminded, giving her a peck on the cheek.

Gabriel lounged by the piano smoking a cigar, a little remote from the rest, but looking very pleased with himself, she thought, suddenly irritated.

'I'll get your coat Andrea, and drive you home. You can't drive tonight.'

The coat dropped around her shoulders. The cloakroom must have been unheated. She shivered. There was the slap of cold air. Darkness. The rustle of paper and dust like the patter of tiny feet. Dirty scraps of newspaper curling around her ankles. Closed and shuttered shops. Rubbish in the gutters. Smell of rotting vegetables. High heels clattering on the pavement.

'Here's the car. Get in.' She felt his hard fingers through the coat, the welcoming softness of the seat, a glimpse of trees in a lamplit square.

Her head fell back and she was aware of fleeting sensations. Slam of doors.

The scent of sandalwood. Revving engine. Nausea as the car reversed, then jerked forward. Forcing her heavy eyes apart she saw Big Ben's hands at 2.15 and deserted Westminster Bridge. Her eyes closed.

★　★　★

An icy blast — a firm hand tugging her arm. The slam of doors. Reluctantly she left the warm interior of the car and allowed herself to be led across the pavement into the entrance hall. Was it her footsteps thundering on the stairs? When he took the key from her hand his eyes looked down into hers, whites glinting in the dark.

She kicked off her shoes and his body rose three inches. 'Are you pleased with me Gabby?' she murmured into the white frill on his shirt.

Feeling very daring at calling him Gabby, she exalted in the freedom of intoxication. An excuse to behave as she would. Irresponsible. The champagne would be blamed for anything she did tonight. An exciting thought.

'Gabby, Gabby, Gabby.' She hiccupped.

His arms went around her, his hands hard against her rib cage. He kicked her shoes into the room and she felt his muscles tense against her weight.

He moved awkwardly, pressing down the light switch with his elbow so that the room flooded with light. Blinking, and aware of emotions raging through her body, she hid her burning face against his shoulder. Not until she was being lowered gently on to the settee did she open her eyes to see Gabriel towering above her and beyond him, the gaping door and the dark landing.

A mixture of fear and excitement shot through her body. 'Close the door Gabby.'

With a few strides he was across the room. 'I will. Good night darling, sleep well.' The door closed gently behind him.

Andrea lay still, not knowing why, she

felt like crying. 'The most exciting light of my nife,' she told unsmiling, blank walls. They started to move towards her. 'The most excsh . . . '

* * *

'Come in.' Andrea swivelled around on the dressing-table stool; her face lit up and she motioned towards the old armchair. 'Sit down for a minute Jill.'

Jill dropped elegantly into the chair, folding long legs beneath her; her glance at Andrea was shrewd. 'Bit low tonight luv?'

Andrea shrugged. 'Perhaps. Don't know why.'

Jill looked concerned. 'Do you miss your parents?'

Andrea cleared her throat. 'In a way they took part of my life with them; I never go down to Kent now, so I've lost touch with friends I grew up with and I've had no time to make more. I never see the boys now.'

Jill raised her eyebrows. 'You must

get hundreds of invitations. We imagined you out somewhere every night.'

'Unless I'm prepared to go out with strangers who turn up at the stage door — and I'm not — who else do I see but the company?' Andrea retorted. 'The rest of you meet for dinner after the show . . . ' She felt her face redden.

'I didn't think,' said Jill slowly, 'you'd want to come out with us and as for the others . . . there might also be . . . '

'What?'

'Well, jealousy Andy. Don't forget that you're Gabriel's protégée. We just work here and we're necessary as long as we're good enough to make his show a success; if we aren't then there are others who are. But you're an individual, even more important to him than the show. It's bound to set you apart.'

Andrea threw up her hands. 'See what I mean?'

'I know.' Jill's voice rang with sympathy. 'And the fellas think you're already spoken for.'

51

'Ha! That's funny. Who have they paired me up with?'

'Gabriel, of course. They see you as his private property. They wouldn't dare ask you out.'

'You're joking! He doesn't know I exist off stage.'

Jill looked thoughtful. 'I'm relieved to hear it.'

'Why?'

'I thought . . . you liked him. I know you once fought, but lately you're more friendly, and you both go off alone after the show. We jumped to the conclusion . . .'

'That we're going out together,' Andrea finished acidly.

Jill shrugged. 'You say it isn't true, so . . .'

'Honestly Jill, you know how he treats me at times, hardly like a lover . . .'

Jill shook her head. 'That could be put down to sheer professionalism, nothing less than anyone would expect from Mr Gabriel Fox.'

Andrea sighed. 'I couldn't stand him at one time, yet . . . I don't know. I owe him a lot.'

'He's a dark horse Andy. We know nothing about his private life, and the press hardly mentions him, apart from some write-ups when you first joined him.' Jill laughed. 'And pictures of you singing together, gazing into each other's eyes.'

'I'm a talented actress too,' retorted Andrea. 'Didn't you know?'

Jill grinned. 'We don't even know if he's married, or where he lives . . . ' She paused. 'Do you?'

Andrea's face fell. 'I hoped you'd know something about him. I think he lives in Kent. I was going to Rochester once to visit the parents and I saw him turning off the A2 somewhere.'

'The mystery man.' Jill uncurled her legs and stretched. 'He never mentions a wife or family; he comes alone to all the parties. Yet how can a man like that be free? For all his faults, he is attractive, for an older man, and he has a lovely long, lean body.' She winked.

Andrea smiled, shaking her head. 'I assure you I never see him outside the theatre.'

Jill heaved herself from the armchair and put an arm around Andrea's shoulders.

'Cheer up luv. Tonight I have a date, but how about coming back to my place for dinner after the show tomorrow? Oh, tomorrow's Sunday. Make it Monday then.'

'Thanks Jill. Don't be late for your date now.' Andrea, unable to remember the last time she'd had a heart to heart talk with another girl, felt refreshed, her mood more buoyant and optimistic.

Jill glanced at her watch. 'Christ, look at the time. See you Monday.'

Andrea watched her go and turned back to the mirror, massaging and wiping until not a scrap of make-up, or any part of the wistful expression remained.

★ ★ ★

She slid into the driver's seat, slammed the door and turned the ignition key. The engine coughed — and went silent. Feeling her face drain of colour, Andrea looked around.

The barely lit car-park, stinking of rubber, petrol and damp, resembled a vast mucky underworld. The grey concrete pillars were thick enough to hide a man.

Again and again she turned the key, hearing the echo of that sickly cough; even that, though, was better than silence, because here it was hard to believe the city of London roared overhead. No other cars lay idly on the wide stretch of concrete; they and their owners had long since rejoined the world. What then, lurked behind the pillars? Whose footfalls pattered in her imagination?

She pulled the choke — the engine growled.

'You beast.' She felt like getting out

and aiming a vicious kick at the gleaming bodywork.

Suddenly there came a tapping on the window.

Andrea froze.

5

'Gabriel!' She wound down the window.

'Trouble?'

'The damn thing won't start.'

'Afraid I know nothing about engines,' he drawled.

He didn't have to sound so pleased. He seemed to go out of his way to be uncooperative where she was concerned. She clenched her teeth. 'What can I do then?'

Assuming a mask of indifference, he hesitated. 'I suppose I could give you a lift to Blackheath and on Monday I'll have it towed to a garage.'

'Thanks for the gracious offer,' she snapped. 'I'll arrange the garage — just get me home. I'm fed up.'

He yanked open the door. 'Out you get then.'

Feeling the dankness thrown out by

concrete walls and conscious of the clatter of her heels she followed his long stride across the dark cavern where his black Morris was partly hidden by a pillar.

While he walked around to unlock the driver's door she was tempted to open the glove compartment and see if it contained anything. A lacy handkerchief maybe, or a lipstick. But before she could give way to her curiosity he was opening the door and seating himself beside her.

It was strange, being close to him in that small space. His hand actually scraped her thigh when he reached for the gear stick, but he didn't seem to notice. The well-behaved car climbed up towards the bright lights and still crowded streets of London, and was soon crossing Westminster Bridge.

'Look at the time, nearly midnight already. Won't your wife be wondering where you are?'

She glanced at his profile, but he kept his eyes on the road ready to negotiate a roundabout. Her question hung in the air like an echo and when at last the reply came her spirits dived to the floor.

'My wife . . . is away at the moment.'

'Oh.' She swallowed a great lump in her throat. Curiosity killed the cat, she could hear her mother saying many times over the years as Andrea's urgent need to know got her into yet another scrape. You've certainly inherited your father's nose for a mystery, girl, was a comment which made her father laugh and pat her on the shoulder.

The remainder of the journey passed in silence until Gabriel pulled up outside a wine bar, switched off the engine and turned towards her.

From the light of a lantern she saw his face crinkle into a smile, and there was a glow in his eyes that she couldn't have described but somehow made her catch her breath.

'Don't know about you, but I'm hungry,' he said. 'Do you think they'll still serve us?'

She smiled back, feeling herself flood

with warmth. 'They're friends of mine. I often eat here late.'

There were maybe only a dozen tables and chairs squashed together, with candles in amber pots creating cosy little islands. Soft music played and delicious scents of wine and cream, tomatoes and herbs sent Andrea's stomach into a gurgle of delight. She could never eat before the show.

Mario placed her favourite wine on the table. 'How did it go tonight?'

She smiled up at him. 'Very well I think.'

'She's good Mario,' said Gabriel, 'a star.'

'Not yet,' she laughed. But her heart pounded. What a man. Insults one minute, compliments the next. Who was the real Gabriel? What did he really think of her? She was vividly reminded of the last time they ate dinner together, on the night they met. She had been puzzled by him then, she recalled. Now, nearly a year later, she was no wiser. He was still an enigma.

A mystery man.

He was leaning back in the chair watching her through half closed eyes. How could I have despised him so much? she wondered. I'll be careful tonight, I mustn't spoil an evening like this.

'You suffer badly from stage fright,' he stated.

Startled, she could only nod.

He toyed with his omelette. 'It's making you jumpy, and emotional. Perhaps I can help.'

Andrea sipped wine. 'Gabriel, I've tried everything.'

'Not everything. I have a friend who's a psychiatrist; he had helped . . . people I know.'

She made herself turn his words over in her mind before answering; with her fork hovering over the lasagne she leaned towards him, allowing her eyes to linger on his face. 'I would appreciate your help.'

Surprise flickered in his eyes. Did he expect me to jump down his throat, she asked herself? Then, discomforted, she remembered the times she had done just that, and perhaps the war hadn't been entirely on his side after all. Could it be that her jumpiness and irritability lately had contributed?

Lulled by the new togetherness, the wine and the deserted room, she began to talk.

'It's not what I thought it would be . . . '

'Oh?' He pushed away his empty plate and touched the end of his cigar to the candle.

She breathed in aromatic smoke. 'I should be feeling great. I'm happy out there, on stage, once I get started, yet when I come off I drop like a stone.' Her brow furrowed. 'It's as if I'm searching for something.'

'Searching? Thanks Mario.' He smiled up at the man and looked back at Andrea. Eyes narrowed against the smoke, he rocked a bulbous glass in his hand.

The golden pool in the bottom of the

glass slurped backwards and forwards. 'For something to keep me going until I get back on stage,' she said desperately.

He threw back his head, lifted the glass. His throat moved, the smell of brandy floated between them — she waited for the understanding reply.

With a thud, the glass hit the table; he stubbed out his cigar and pushed back his chair. The amazing crinkles swept up his face.

He slid a wallet from his pocket. 'Don will sort you out.'

She sighed deeply.

*　*　*

Standing in the dark outside her flat Andrea watched the tail lights of his car disappear towards the A2, dancing before her like red eyes. What a splendid evening. She wouldn't think about his wife, just concentrate upon the new friendship that had been formed between them.

She crept up the polished stairs, past two landings of closed doors, letting herself into her flat and quietly closing the door. This was the most depressing time of day. Her neighbours left for work before she was up in the mornings, and were asleep behind closed doors when she returned. Although exhausted when she left the theatre, by the time she reached home she was usually unready for bed.

With little enthusiasm she prepared a hot drink, and on her way through the lounge to the bedroom stopped at the coffee table to pick up that week's copy of *Stage*. She never knew afterwards why she also pulled a telephone directory from the pile and took it with her.

She sat up in bed reading. Her finger ran down the flimsy page — Farrow, Fawcett, Field, Fox — Gabriel Peter Fox, Tanglewood, Lower Oakfield, Kent.

★　★　★

Andrea watched anxiously as he looked inside the engine. Presently he walked towards her, wiping his hands on a rag.

'Ignition fault, take about three days.'

'Damn! Thanks for looking at it for me on a Sunday, Jim. I'll collect it on Wednesday then.'

'Rightho.' He accompanied her to the garage entrance. 'Looks like rain.'

Miserably she looked up at the troubled, slate grey sky. 'I was hoping to drive out to Kent today.'

He held out his hand, catching the first spots of rain. 'Not much of a Sunday for it.'

'No. Not much of a Sunday.'

★ ★ ★

She was soaking in the bath watching the lather settle into meringue nests, and listening to a Sunday evening concert on the radio when the telephone rang.

'Oh hell.'

Clambering out she grasped a towel

and sped into the lounge, struggling to cover her cold shoulders with the towel and pull the phone from the hook.

'Andrea?'

'Gabriel?' I was just thinking about you, she almost said, but stopped herself in time. She listened to his voice, watching the beige carpet at her feet darken. 'Tomorrow evening? By train, the car's in the garage until Wednesday.'

I wonder what it's like at Tanglewood now, she thought. Mushy and brown with autumn leaves, I expect.

'Sorry Gabriel, what did you say? That's very good of you. Smashing. Yes, I'll be downstairs on the dot. Four o'clock. Thanks again for ringing. Bye.'

Reluctantly she put the receiver down and returned to the bathroom, smiling brightly and foolishly at her steamy reflection in the mirror.

★ ★ ★

Andrea settled back in the car. 'Did you enjoy your Sunday? How is your wife?'

'You're chirpy this evening,' he replied.

'It's good to be going back,' she explained simply.

Pulling away from the kerb he glanced sideways. 'You've been away for one day; does it mean that much?'

'Mm. When I'm in the wings waiting to go on I think why am I going through this terror? I'll give it up. You know what I mean?'

'Indeed I do. I've seen it so many times.'

The grey stone church slipped backwards and was hidden behind a fold of green common as they went down the hill past the shops. There was a blaze of colour from fruit, vegetables and flowers. They were passing the sleeping wine bar when Gabriel reached out with his left hand and flipped open the glove compartment. Before she could see what was inside he had closed it and was dropping a card into her lap.

67

Ignoring it, she went on, 'Going on stage is a sort of outlet — freedom to sing it out. When I leave the stage the lights inside me go out.' She laughed brightly. 'Look — it's a bit like being an electric plug; when I'm connected to the theatre I'm fizzing with life, when I'm disconnected the power goes.'

I'm gabbling, she thought, when he made no reply. Shut up Andrea, he's obviously not interested. With a sigh she threw herself back against the seat and watched the unreal world outside slip smoothly past.

The day had never really got light and the late afternoon hung over the Old Kent Road like a faded, yellowing net curtain, turning the walls of lanky Victorian houses to brass.

Andrea was thankful for the glass that separated her from the dismal outside. They passed a sour brown public house, the betting shop with veiled windows; and everywhere, the rubbish. Newspaper, cigarette packets, empty cans and bottles whirled across the road, fluttering into the kerb and on to the pavements — an eddying mael-strom of left-overs.

Despite the heater, she shivered. Could this be the stem of her fear? That failure could turn her into a piece of rubbish in a grey street? There were no stars in her eyes, she had her father's practical nature. She knew the precari-ousness of her chosen profession, and that it was a very short journey from where she was now, to that world outside. There were no guarantees, no pension, no insurances and no miracles.

'Andrea.' His voice broke her reverie. 'This is Don's number. Give him a ring. I'm sure he'll help.'

She looked down at the card in her lap.

'You said on Saturday you'd go,' he snapped.

In the terse reminder she recognized the strain reappearing between them, and wondered at it. They could only be together for such a short time before this curtain of tension sprang up.

She seethed with indignation. 'I never break promises.'

'Don't forget then. It's for your own good.'

'Stop treating me like a child!'

He laughed, swerving to overtake a car. 'My dear girl . . . '

Turning her face away she sang a few bars of her latest number beneath her breath, enjoying his irritation.

The Houses of Parliament came into view and then Big Ben was looking down on the surging carousel of vehicles. Gabriel manoeuvred into the traffic clawing its way around Parliament Square.

The journey was almost over.

★   ★   ★

In her dressing-room she switched on the electric fire and sank deep into the lumpy old armchair, trying to forget the sneer on Jill's face when she broke their dinner engagement. 'My car's in the garage and Gabriel is giving me a lift home,' she had explained.

'That's up to you,' had been the terse reply.

Andrea sighed. Forget Jill, she told herself. So she went over in her mind the words to the three songs she was to sing, thankful for her good memory. Her main problem was nerves, and she suddenly realized that she still clutched Gabriel's card in her hand. She tossed it into her handbag. It was time to get ready.

The bulbs around the mirror seemed to waver as she wiped her clammy hands with a tissue and started to put on her make-up.

'Beginners please,' echoed through the corridor.

She slipped the bandeau from her hair and pressed in the waves with her hand.

'Let it grow,' Gabriel had ordered. 'It accentuates your femininity, your smooth rather than jerky movements.'

'Five minutes Miss Grace.'

Leaning against the door she took a deep breath. The sallow-walled room now looked enticingly cosy in the glow of the fire. She stepped out into the chilly corridor.

6

'I won't have time for a meal tonight.' His voice was curt, his gaze steady on the rain-lashed road.

Miserably she wondered why the atmosphere was so different from last time. Did he think that she expected to be taken for a meal every time he gave her a lift home? What a cheek! Who does he think he is?

'Your wife will have your meal ready, I suppose,' she said sweetly.

'Why did you change that last note in 'Starless Nights'?' he demanded.

He always does that, she fumed. Acts as if I haven't spoken. She made her voice cool. 'I decided it sounds better up than down.'

The light turned to amber. 'I think you forgot,' he snapped, and the car shot around the roundabout towards Elephant and Castle.

'What did it matter?' she taunted. 'You leave me as the music fades. It's my note.'

'Grow up Andrea, you're in the theatre now, not some twopenny halfpenny pub.'

She watched the wipers parting the curtain of water, aware that everything was off key between them, and knowing herself to be in the wrong. She *had* forgotten.

Wrapped in their own thoughts they passed the wine bar and the church and turned into the street where she lived. Casting a glance at his grim profile from beneath her lashes, her spirits plummeted. She had only tolerated his rudeness for the sake of her career, otherwise she would have told him to go to hell long ago. And yet — it had felt good, being friends, she thought bleakly.

'Would you like to come up for a drink?'

Despite his crooked smile the brooding look in his eyes remained. 'Thanks darling, but I have to get home. Same time tomorrow?'

Her muttered yes was lost as she slammed the door with all her might and sloshed around to the pavement.

'Andrea.'

He wound down the window. 'Apart from that note . . . you were good. I'm proud of you.'

Her legs turned to jelly and she leaned against the lamp-post with her heart doing a jig. Beneath the light his eyes glittered with that strange glow.

With a curt goodnight he drove sedately away, and again she watched the twin red spots being swallowed up by the darkness of the early morning common.

But he did smile, she thought, as she switched off the light and lay her head on the pillow. Very fleeting, but he did smile.

★   ★   ★

'Oh no, Jim, you said the car would be ready today.'

'Didn't know what else I'd find, did I, love?'

'When will it be ready then?'

He pursed his lips. 'Next Monday.'

'But I need it for the weekend!'

He puffed at the skinny cigarette. 'You could hire one. There's a car hire place three doors down.'

'I'll do that.' Andrea marched out of the garage and turned into the High Street. 'I can manage on weekdays; I just need it for the weekend,' she told the girl behind the desk.

The girl smiled. 'Collect Saturday, return Monday.'

★　★　★

She recognized Gabriel's broad back as she sped through the corridor; he was about to enter his room.

'Gabriel.'

He turned with an abstracted smile. 'Shall I meet you in the car-park

76

later?' she asked.

His black brows drew together. 'I thought you'd have your own car. I've made other arrangements.'

With an irritated shuffle of the papers he held in his hand, he shrugged and went inside, slamming the door behind him.

In the dressing-room her eyes blazed into the mirror and she brushed her hair until it crackled. 'Let it grow, Andrea,' he had ordered. 'It suits you better. Short hair only accentuates your pointed nose.'

She slammed down the hairbrush and was rummaging in the drawer for scissors when someone rapped on the door.

'Come in,' she yelled.

'Hear you're stuck for a lift tonight.' Len swung a trombone in his hand and met her frown with a lopsided grin. 'I've come to offer my services, ma'am.'

'Did Gabriel ask you to offer me a lift?'

His grin faded and he cleared his

throat. 'He said you were stuck without a car. It's really not far out of my way and we might stop for a bite to eat.'

'That would be lovely, I know just the place, a dear little wine bar not far from my flat . . . oh, hullo Gabriel.'

'Have you made that appointment?'

She lifted her chin. 'I'm going on Monday.'

'Good girl. See you on stage. Good luck.'

'Beginners please,' came the call.

Gabriel disappeared, leaving them staring mutely after him.

'He's got 'em tonight,' Len grimaced.

Andrea smiled grimly.

'Don't understand him,' Len muttered. 'He's a good friend to anyone in trouble but his black moods . . . whew! Anyway — I must go.'

The assistant stage manager put his head around the door. 'Thirty minutes Miss Grace.'

The door slammed and she was alone.

Alone to do battle with her fears; to

push back the rising tide of sickness; to feel her knees tremble against taffeta dressing-table frills and her hand shake as she held the crayon to her eyes.

★ ★ ★

Andrea chatted brightly on the way home, determined not to admit to herself how much she missed Gabriel. The smell of him, his immense body filling the car so that his thigh just brushed hers; the warmth of him and the glow of energy that radiated from him.

An air of unreality accompanied her into the wine bar. She sat at the same table; the same music sent prickles up and down her spine; the smell of spices and herbs, cream and tomatoes wafted from the kitchen, as before. And the candle flickered in the little amber pot, as before. Only now she felt desolate and empty.

Len's voice came from a distance.

'Coming back to what we were saying . . . '

'Oh. Sorry. Yes?'

'About Gabriel. Don't take it personally. He's had these moods ever since I've known him.'

'How long is that Len?'

'Three years. A friend of mine was with his first band; he told me a bit about him.'

Andrea's heart beat faster. 'Tell me.'

'When Gabriel was fourteen his father died; he sort of took his mother under his wing, became a dead loss with his mates, I understand. Always working after school.'

Andrea sliced through the cannelloni. 'What about his wife?'

'She was at school with him I believe. But Mike didn't say much about her.' He reached out to refill her glass. 'In fact no one talked about her and I felt that the subject was taboo. Probably the marriage broke up.'

Andrea watched bubbles surge to the surface of her drink. Then in a low voice she started to sing to the music. 'You go to my head . . . like sparkling champagne,' and Len joined in until they were overtaken by laughter.

Soon they were involved in a friendly discussion and she was surprised how well the time could pass when you're trying to entertain someone. Acting, in other words. The wine helped too, of course.

'You know, you're different from what I expected,' he confided, over coffee.

'In what way?'

'I thought you were cold and ambitious; truculent sometimes, and immature. You've plenty of spunk; you don't let anyone sit on you, but you can be so off hand . . . '

She lifted her cup and gulped down cold coffee that tasted as bitter as her feelings. 'Is that how I appear?'

He nodded. 'But the real you is young and gay; you're different when you laugh and act like a kid. Your trouble is that you've had to grow up too soon. You're being pushed into a sophisticated role I don't think you're ready for.'

She lifted her chin. 'Gabriel does.'

Len shrugged. 'You've a mature voice. But . . . you're in the right place at the wrong time.'

He beckoned to Mario and turned back to Andrea. 'And you're kidding yourself. I know you're ambitious, but the theatre isn't your life as you keep saying it is. It's only half of it. You need to fill the other half.'

He waved some bank notes in the air. 'Thanks Mario.'

'Did Gabriel order you to give me a lecture as well as a ride home?' she asked sourly.

He reached out for her hand. 'Lovey, you've got it wrong. I've enjoyed myself; loved your company. You're nicer than I ever imagined. I admit, when Gabriel asked me I thought it a chore, but now that we've had a chance to get to know each other . . . '

She snatched her hand away. 'Seeing

as this is truth night, Leonard, I've no intention of getting to know you better, and I wanted a lift from you about as much as you wanted to give it.'

Standing up, she leaned across the table and patted his flabby cheek. 'But I too had a better time than I expected. Even though you, as a much older man, felt it necessary to pass on your experience as a very old pro.'

She couldn't understand why she let him kiss her goodnight in the entrance hall; but people did it all the time, a kiss meant nothing.

I'll prove I'm no ice maiden, she thought, ignoring the unpleasant tickle from his moustache. But her mind wandered. Does Gabriel think the same about me?

Firmly she shoo'd Len away when he would have climbed the stairs. Suddenly she felt tired and awash with wine.

For the first time she didn't remove her make-up — her clothes lay where they fell. She forgot to close the curtains and the big white-faced church clock on the dark common outside her bedroom showed 4.15 when she switched out the light and lay down to sleep, feeling blessedly comfortable and released from tension.

For she had made up her mind what to do on Sunday.

★　★　★

Warm fingers of sunshine stroked her face, pulling her from sleep. Moaning, she turned her head the other way. It wasn't until church bells began their doleful clanging that she opened her eyes to see the clock staring at her through uncurtained windows. Eleven o'clock.

Startled, she sat up in bed. Today she was going to find Tanglewood. A sliver of excitement told her she had made the right decision; she had never enjoyed aimless Sundays; she needed anticipation to start her day the way some needed that first coffee.

Beyond the window stretches of grass extended like a carpet from the road to the park wall. Multi-coloured kites were pitching and rolling and soaring into a cloudless sky, while down below crisp brown leaves chased each other into kerbs and fluttered across pavements.

An untidy day. A day for doing, not sitting.

* * *

'Follow the yellow brick road,' she sang. Grey tarmac rushed forward and slipped beneath the car as she sped along. Glancing in the mirror, she sidled into the lefthand lane. Somewhere here was where Gabriel had turned off. Spinning wheels and thundering engines gave way to stillness and silence; trees closed around her, stifling light; she was cruising beneath a roof of entwined branches. In the diffused light the signpost that showed Lower Oakwood was barely discernible.

The lane, spotted with sunlight and

littered with leaves and chestnuts, twisted and turned below high banks and hedgerows where blowsy blackberries and crimson berries tangled with the last of the honey-suckle. Rabbits bounded from her path and disappeared into undergrowth; jackdaws hopped on to the road and flew away just as she reached them as if playing 'dare'.

The banks either side were now higher than the car, leaving the knotty roots of great trees exposed, giving the eerie sensation of travelling through an underworld. A prickle ran up and down her spine. What sort of mess had she got herself into now?

You're stubborn Andrea, her mother used to say. When you make up your mind to do something you won't give in.

After passing three secluded driveways, none of which displayed the name she was looking for, she came across the village. A pond with houses on three sides and a public house on the other.

She pulled into the kerb. What to do now she was here?

Supposing he came along and saw her there? What would he think? She was just out for a Sunday afternoon drive? Sure. Just coincidence I chose this particular village, she taunted herself. Then she tossed her head. It was quite natural to be curious about where he lived.

I'll walk, she decided, locking the car.

She discovered a tiny path winding away from the centre of the village. Here she found a butcher, a baker, a general store and a twelfth century church. And further on a cottage that looked like something from a fairy-tale.

The roof was firmly thatched, not a hair out of place. Tiny windows twinkled like eyes beneath hooded thatch lids, and downstairs were another three latticed windows, two on one side of the door and one on the other. The walls were painted pink, and the paintwork on doors and window frames was blue. Pale, dusty colours, like a child's picture in chalk.

Larger than she had first supposed, it must, she realized, have at least four bedrooms, two of them up in the eaves.

A small garden at the front spread wide at the sides and a glimpse of tousled tree heads — brown, gold and green — suggested it was probably far reaching at the back. Tangled woodlands surrounded the cottage on three sides. Yellowish smoke rose from the chimney.

Andrea smiled. There was always something interesting to see if you leave home and walk. That, she had learned as an only child needing to make her own amusement. Now she dawdled along the fence, breathing with relish the delicious, evocative scent of woodsmoke. The gate was painted blue.

The name there said quite clearly — Tanglewood.

Disbelief was her first reaction. She had expected something quite different. But there might not only be Gabriel, she reminded herself. A wife lived there once, perhaps still did. If not a wife, she thought — if he had divorced as gossip supposed — then a mistress, hence the secrecy. Of course, that's the answer.

Stop gawping, fool, she muttered to herself. And strode on.

When the front fence ended she turned into woods. The path led alongside a fenced garden and she followed it to the back of the house.

She realized the incongruity of her actions very well, yet she had arrived there not under her own volition but impelled by a force like gravity. He was her link with the theatre, she supposed, a bridge from the hated Sunday to Monday evening. Now she stared up at the house with mixed feelings. She was at the moment in a no man's land, neither with him, yet not as far away as usual, which suddenly she realized was the most important thing. At the same time her frustration and helplessness made the loss of him more unbearable, and she gasped at the desolation and pain of standing there, outside his life.

What a fool she had been to come. What on earth had come over her?

Turning away, she came face to face with Gabriel.

7

The logs he was carrying fell to the ground. She stared as if mesmerized at his wellington boots and baggy checked trousers, hardly recognizing the svelte man she knew. He looks, she thought, like a giant teddy bear in that cream sweater.

A pulse beat madly in her throat as she waited for the outburst of anger, forgetting, in her guilt, that he had no idea of her plotting to get there. What would he do? What would he say?

It must only have been seconds that they stood there staring at each other, yet it seemed longer before he stepped forward. The hands that reached out and curled around hers were warm.

'It gets cold early this time of year,' he said softly.

Swallowing the lump in her throat, she ran her tongue around her dry lips, feeling as vulnerable as she had as a child after being discovered in a prank.

And then his arms were opening wide and she was wrapped inside them. So familiar, so strong, so tenderly protective; squeezing her as if to pull her into his own body; lifting her from her feet. Her face was crushed against his sweater, his hand pressed on her hair.

She heard a whisper, 'Andy, Andy my love.'

When she raised her face his cold cheek was against hers; his stubbled chin rubbed and pressed and nudged, pushing her face around to where his warm mouth waited. Their lips clung together, yet his kiss was gentle and exploratory; every nerve in her body scrambled to reach that one spot. Nerve end to nerve end, body to body, they stood together in their own magic circle of homecoming.

When at last they moved apart, Andrea found herself standing on trembling tiptoes with his arms still supporting her. She felt the hammering of his heart beneath her hand. He smelled of cold, fresh air.

'Darling,' he said in a voice husky and so unlike his own. 'What brings you here?'

She had smashed, suddenly and unexpectedly into a wall of passion that left her shaking and shocked. Yet her heart lurched in a sea of joy such as she had never known. So within him she could only remain still, with no longings to confess. Resting there against the soft wool of his sweater she listened as his heart, like her own, began to slow down.

His chin rested on her hair. 'Were you lonely Andy?'

Sensing her reluctance to talk, he asked tenderly, 'Did you come to find me because you're lonely?'

'It was a lovely day,' she muttered at last. 'Not a day for being in.' It was as if she had been tossed by a boiling sea on to the sand, and lay there stranded — gasping and disorientated.

'I worry about you.' His lips gently pressed against her hair and he breathed deeply. 'Your hair smells like lemons.'

'Why do you worry?' She searched his eyes.

'You seem to live for the theatre. You're so restless on Saturday night, and overstrung on Mondays. I know you love it but . . . '

'I do.' Her eyes glowed into his, seeking his understanding.

'It's new to you sweetheart, but there's life outside it, and you don't do much living, it seems to me. I feel responsible,' he sighed. 'I've been so wrapped up myself in getting you started, I've not encouraged you to think of anything else. To be honest, perhaps I didn't want you to, I was being possessive and selfish. But now you should be able to relax a little.'

The sun disappeared behind a swirling mass of grey cloud and the trees began to lose their colour and take on the blackness of evening.

She had a sense of foreboding, resentfully aware that his words were scattering the joy. All men wanted to do was lecture her, it seemed. 'Why didn't you say anything then, like ask me out?'

In the silence she felt warmth rush to her face. 'I mean — if you were that worried,' she added weakly.

A bird threw out notes of piercing sweetness and the wood-notes — the crackle of twigs, the rustle of leaves — were suddenly ominous.

To avoid his gaze she looked towards the house. A shadow moved across one of the windows. But the setting sun had pushed, as if taking a last bow, through billowing clouds, and blazed like fire on the glass. So she couldn't be sure.

With an edge to his voice he answered her question. 'I'm not free to ask you. I have a wife.'

She broke away from his embrace, leaving his hands to fall to his sides. 'I thought,' she laughed jerkily, 'it was because you didn't like me. You did say I was plain.'

He chuckled then and she wondered how he could laugh when a tragedy was being acted out.

'I said I knew many more glamorous women. True. They're two a penny. You though, my love, have an extra something that twined itself around my heart.' His voice sank. 'Something I had to fight to stay free from.'

His eyes were opaque with tenderness, his voice vibrating with emotion. 'Those piercing brown eyes of yours — as dark as chestnuts, and vibrantly alive. They fasten on to whoever you're talking to, or listening to and one drowns there. The way your cheek curves like a child's, and your little pointed nose gives a quiver when you laugh. Your tempers! You're five feet nothing, yet to see you stand up for yourself . . . ' He shook his head, giving a boyish grin.

But the grin faded as he looked at the house. 'I don't know what to do now.'

Gabriel at a loss, and with a tremor in his voice!

'What do you mean?' she frowned.

'You're miles from home. It's getting dark and cold. I yearn to wrap you in my arms and take you in by the fire.' He shook his head, sounding surprised. 'It's a most frustrating sensation. But I can't take you in. And I really must go.'

Jealousy spat like fire in her chest and she stood ramrod straight.

'I have a car — it won't take me long to get home.'

Something curled inside her at the look of relief he couldn't hide. What did she expect? That he would walk out on his wife there and then?

Andrea allowed herself a brief fantasy — he would drive her home and stay with her in the flat. She despised herself, yet longed with all her heart that it could have been that way, aching to be wrapped in his arms again, where she had felt safe and warm, yet wondering how she could feel so. This wasn't how it was meant to be today; a man's arms weren't the be all and the end all of a woman's life any more.

Yet — she couldn't deny that it had been a feeling like nothing she had ever known, a homecoming, a strange fulfilment of an aching need.

Sickened by the longing to stay, she turned away.

His fingers grasped her arm. 'Andy. You do understand, darling, don't you?'

She fought to control her voice. 'Of course. You didn't ask me to come here. I wanted somewhere to go, that's all.' Her voice broke. 'It was a nice day . . . '

'Don't Andy. Don't.'

His voice, soft and coaxing as she had rarely heard it, touched a spring of emotion she couldn't check, and she spun round to face him. 'I suppose you wish I hadn't come . . . ?'

With a thumping heart and a desperate ache to be once more in his arms, she waited for his denial.

His hand fell to his side, his eyes gazed bleakly back at her. 'It might have been better for both of us.'

She gasped as his words ripped through her like bullets, leaving behind a devastating soreness. But she still, before she turned and walked away, managed to throw him a look of contempt. She took with her the loneliness of the woods, the birds' plaintive evensong, and the stillness of Gabriel as he stood with his hands by his sides, his shoulders bowed and a look on his face of helpless longing.

8

Andrea was half-heartedly pushing the vacuum cleaner backwards and forwards when the telephone rang.

Quick pips were followed by the unmistakable deep and abrupt voice of Gabriel.

'Andy? I'm in a call box in the village.'

The one by the pond, she remembered with a pang.

'Andy? Are you there? I must see you before the show. We need to talk. Let's meet somewhere.'

With a shiver of delight she glanced around the room and down at her shabby jeans. 'You can come here.'

'No. Somewhere outside. What about the tea room in the park? About one o'clock?'

His caution touched a raw nerve. 'Right. See you then,' she snapped.

A burst of pips, a clatter as the receiver went down, and he was gone — leaving her staring at the silent telephone wishing she had sounded more pleasant.

She had half an hour. Shoving the vacuum cleaner to one side she rushed to the bathroom, stepped quickly into scented bathwater and out again, dried herself and dusted on talcum. Then she was speeding towards the bedroom.

There was a crash of hangers — numerous pairs of jeans rattled out of sight into the depths of the wardrobe; she wrenched out a smart trouser suit and tossed it on to the bed. The red dress she had bought to wear last Christmas? Too bright. Impatiently she flicked it to one side.

Her mother's voice rang in her ears. 'Another pair of jeans Andrea? For someone who wants to be on the stage, you take no interest in your appearance whatever'. At the thought of her mother's wardrobe, with its pretty dresses, suits and blouses, Andrea groaned.

Into view rattled a navy two piece, bought for an audition once. She yanked it out and held it against her. The skirt flared to just above her knees; the collar of the jacket was sailor style. With a matching pair of navy blue shoes and handbag, she felt quite prim and brittle, just as she wanted to feel.

She pulled a face at herself in the mirror. The night had obviously been spent tossing and turning, cringing with shame at the soft, emotional girl of yesterday.

The church clock told her she still had ten minutes to go and she chivvied the vacuum cleaner into the cupboard, and tidied up records and items of clothing that were scattered around the lounge. Back in the bedroom she decided after all to just accentuate her eyes with a touch of blue liner and grey shadow. Perhaps some of that navy blue mascara too. Studying herself she added pale lipstick, then rubbed it off.

He might kiss her again.

A frisson of excitement darted through her body setting her face flaming. How could she allow her emotions to be so out of control?

A glance in the mirror showed shining eyes and pink cheeks, and she turned away from the balmy rooms to see what awaited her in the antiseptic autumn sunshine.

The tea house was perched on a hill overlooking Greenwich and the Thames.

Gabriel was already there, sitting outside in the sunshine with the collar of his jacket turned up and the breeze ruffling his hair.

Her feet crunched over a carpet of dying leaves as she made her way between white plastic tables and chairs towards him. Suddenly she was shy. His smile was both welcoming and uncertain; his hesitant kiss merely a meeting of lips, and her heart twisted into a knot.

'Hi, Gabby.'

'Hello sweetheart. What can I get you?'

She searched his face, saying the first thing that came into her head. 'Ploughman's and coffee please.'

In an agony of suspense she watched him duck his head to go through the door.

Birds pecked around her feet, searching soggy leaves for crumbs. Far below, at the bottom of the green hill, the creamy pillars of Greenwich Palace stood beside the Thames. Sunshine stroked the river with silver, turning daylight to shimmering old gold, as only an autumn sun in England can. It seemed that nothing moved, neither the pin-sized boats on the river, nor spirals of smoke from factory chimneys. As if even life held its breath.

She shivered, touched by fingers of the future, looking back on herself, and knowing instinctively that in future years autumn, especially a golden autumn, would remind her of Gabby; that the sight and scent of moribund leaves, woodsmoke and dying sun, would bring upon her a special, wistful melancholy.

Sadness struck like a blow, along with a premonition of disaster. Her father had laughed at her premonitions, her mother, though, understood. Yesterday, before she set off for Tanglewood, she had ignored the warning. Too many things had tried to prevent her from going there. Stubborn — as her mother said.

'Come back Andy. You're miles away.'

Gabriel placed the tray on the table. 'Sure you're warm enough here, we can eat inside?'

She shook her head, wishing she had worn something warmer. 'I feel like some air.'

He arranged plates and a brimming cup of coffee before her while she sat with hands in her lap watching him. He tossed the empty tray on to a nearby table and grunted in satisfaction. 'What were you day-dreaming about?'

She reached out for the cup. 'About

me. The silly things I do sometimes.'

He gave her a piercing look. 'Yesterday, you mean?'

She nodded, balancing the cup in her hands, relishing its warmth. 'Something drove me there.'

'Me calling you, perhaps.'

Her cup crashed into the saucer. 'You're joking.'

He placed a hand over hers. 'Don't you think I miss you on Sundays? Men have their fantasies too, you know.'

Her breath caught in her throat. 'You said . . . you wish it hadn't happened?'

He moved uncomfortably. 'It's a very moving moment when someone you've wanted for so long, and have wearied for, is suddenly there in your arms. Afterwards, must inevitably come . . . confusion.'

Removing his hand he sat back and gazed up into the branches of a chestnut tree. 'I used to fantasize about you walking towards me through the woods, and there you were. But it should never have happened.' His voice deepened. 'I should have had more willpower.'

Andrea stabbed her fork at a square of cheese. One minute his words made her heart leap with delight, the next her stomach churned with misery. 'I thought you might be angry.'

He faced her again, shaking his head. 'Didn't occur to me. I was overjoyed to see you, at first.'

'And then?'

'Then? Then I felt inadequate. Torn. I have an over-protective instinct where women are concerned, I suppose. There you were, someone I love dearly, and I was unable to take care of you. I had to let you go home alone.'

Her heart pounded joyfully. 'You didn't have to.'

A muscle flicked in his cheek. 'My wife . . . '

She felt a whiplash of pain. 'Ah, yes. The invisible wife. The wife no one knew about. You never mention her; I wasn't to know, was I? You ignored my questions.'

His voice was heavy. 'No. You weren't to know.'

Andrea almost relished the spurt of anger she felt. 'Why didn't you tell me?'

He pushed away his plate, reached for cigarettes and matches and slowly lit up. Placing the packet on the table beside his untouched meal, he leaned back and blew smoke into the air.

Andrea waited. He didn't see the small robin hop on to the table and peck at his sandwich. He was looking into the distance.

'We met at school. When Jennifer was fourteen her mother ran away with another man, leaving her with her father, who soon found consolation elsewhere. She enjoyed being at my house; mother felt sorry for her and treated her like the daughter she never had and it seemed natural for us to marry. I ran the college band and when we left college I carried on with it, mostly as a way of keeping the boys together. We called ourselves, not very originally, The Old Boys.' His eyes crinkled and he looked her way.

'We had two guitarists, two tenor saxes, trumpet, organ and surprisingly enough, a lot of bookings. Oh, only the local hops at first, you know. It started out as a hobby but eventually we became so busy we went full time. A bit risky.' He shrugged. 'Gradually we married, had families, and some dropped out. It's a hard life, with little security. Jennifer and I had no children.'

He looked away. There was a young girl — a laughing infant — plump legs toddling over grass — a baby's chuckle — the girl's sheet of black hair as she bent over to pick up a ball. He was watching them, and at the sadness etched on his face, Andrea had to look away.

'It hardly seems possible,' Gabriel went on, 'that two people who knew each other so well, who'd been going out together for seven years, should find, after only a year of marriage, that it wasn't going to work. Yet that's what happened. Incredible.'

He shook his head and stubbed his cigarette into a tin ashtray, raising his eyes to look her in the face. She saw they flickered with disbelief. 'You would have thought, wouldn't you, that a marriage like that would have a better chance of surviving than most?'

Andrea shuddered. I don't want to hear any more, she thought. Not with that expression in his eyes, as if he still cares.

'Jennifer worked hard to help me. She never complained about being hard up — and we were. You wouldn't believe the expense of putting a show on the road. The vehicle, chauffeur-cum-roadie's salary, living expenses; instruments, transport, stage clothes, running overheads. There are the PA systems, the truck for the gear and road crew, the car for the group. Petrol, food, digs, insurances.' He shrugged.

'Anyway, we went on the road, sometimes working until four in the morning; early evening a ballroom, then on to a club. Jennifer collapsed with yellow jaundice brought on by the travelling. She was pregnant, and lost the baby. We were told she wouldn't have another.'

So much bitterness in his voice, thought Andrea, with a surge of pity. His eyes showed such sadness and disillusion that she could have wept. Yet a silent, selfish voice in her head bade him hurry, get to the point, what are you going to do about US?

Gabriel cleared his throat. 'She went to pieces Andy; burning with hatred for me — and my work. Refused to travel with us any more. It was my living by then. What could I do? Mother lived with us, which was useful because I had to leave Jennifer at home. She became housebound — what the doctors call agoraphobic. Mother died eighteen months ago.'

Andrea leaned forward, her eyes clinging to his face, as his voice dropped. 'Last year, while I was away, Jennifer tried to kill herself. She's eaten by jealousy and suspicion, that's her trouble. Even though she could travel with me if she wanted to.'

He saw the question in her eyes, and shook his head. 'She has no one Andy. I'm all she has. Besides, we were happy once. She worked too, to help me get where I am.' Then, bitterly, 'If only I could get through to her.'

Andrea's eyes filled. She was ashamed, knowing that she had wanted to hear a different story, had wanted his wife to be much less than perfect, to have been wanting in fact. Illogically she was furious with herself for having prepared in her mind a ready-made version of his story, and with Gabriel for making his wife sound like a paragon.

But still she was unable to prevent savage fingers of jealousy from probing his feelings. 'You still love her then? You care?'

She was taken aback by the vehemence of his reply, and the rough insistence in his voice. 'Of course I care. I can't remember a time when I didn't.

But I love you. Remember that. Even though I must always look after her,' he said firmly. 'It's my fault, you see — if I hadn't been so ambitious . . . '

Miserably Andrea locked her eyes to his. 'And you don't care about me?'

He leaned forward, picked up her hand and caressed it, pressing on the bones and knuckles, squeezing until she had to stop herself from crying out. 'Of course I care for you,' he said. 'But you can look after yourself. Jennifer can't.'

Andrea wrenched her hand away, enjoying the look of shock on his face. 'Oh I can look after myself. I'm strong and healthy — not an emotional, clinging ivy.'

Hatred of the unknown woman writhed like a demon as she lashed at him in fury until she ran out of words and they both sat white faced, staring at each other.

'Sweetheart . . . ' His voice broke.

With her world crashing around her she stared at the spindly-legged birds hopping between tables — the girl and the baby — a dog fighting a twig — a squirrel begging for nuts — the river meandering onwards.

She watched him through a curtain of wet lashes, her stomach knotting with fear. Realizing that she had reached what she now knew she had been striving for she longed with all her might to keep what she had found. The warmth, the love, the wonder of it.

'What can we do?' she asked.

His face assembled into the stern lines she knew so well. 'What do you want me to say? Give up the stage and be my mistress?'

The blood drained from her face. 'It's . . . not a question of that.'

'Isn't it? How can we work together now? We'll end up destroying each other. Even this afternoon . . . ' He lifted his hands in the air. 'Only yesterday we loved so tenderly and so much. Today — bitterness already.' He nodded. 'If we stay together we lose not only each other but your dream Andy — your dream of stardom.' His hands fell to the table. 'I'm not having your career destroyed or my wife harassed by probing newsmen.'

He lit a cigarette and inhaled deeply. 'I've done my best to protect Jennifer from the press, the least I can do is to allow her to live in peace. Besides, seeing pictures and insinuations about us would fire her jealousy to such an extent I admit I'd fear her reaction.'

'Oh really, Gabby,' she scorned. 'That's a bit dramatic. This is the seventies. I just feel,' — she gave a hysterical laugh — 'that you're making excuses. Don't all you men, in a situation like this?'

A bleak look swept his face. 'You're newsworthy Andy. Remember? You're becoming well known. It would be impossible to keep any liaison between us a secret from the media. There's only one way to avoid publicity, and that's to live like a monk.'

His sardonic smile made him look like the Gabriel she knew, instead of the stranger who sat before her now.

'Monks aren't newsworthy,' he added, with an attempt at humour.

Leaping to her lips before she could stop it was the question she longed to ask. 'Do you still sleep with her?'

'No.' He looked at her steadily. 'That stopped a long time ago. In her muddled way I believe she thinks by refusing to let me make love to her, she's punishing me.' He stubbed out the cigarette and gave a twisted smile. 'She doesn't like me very much.'

The words were torn from her lips. 'So why do you stay with her?'

'Because she's my responsibility,' he barked. 'And because she nearly killed herself once when I suggested she might like a divorce.'

'That's blackmail.'

He shook his head and sounded suddenly tired. 'From my point of view it's concern, pity and . . . a sort of love.'

'Stop it.' she cried. 'I don't want to hear.'

He frowned. 'One day you'll love again. You're so young.'

His words tore her apart; an admission that he didn't want her; confirmation, if confirmation was needed, that he had indeed meant everything he said. How it hurt, she mourned, beyond anything else, when the man you love throws you into the arms of another, even under the guise of sacrifice.

When she shook her head, he added, 'Yes. It will be nothing like you feel for me; it will be different . . . '

She could only stare numbly at him. His face was white, his lips pinched, he looked tired and older. She tried to see down through the transparency of his eyes, searching for the truth and in his worldly-wise way perhaps he saw the doubt and suspicion there.

'Strange, that I,' he said painfully, 'the most faithful and loving of fellows, should only know women who mistrust me.'

Their eyes locked for what seemed an interminable time, then he leaned forward, elbows on the table, hands clasped together. 'If you were not newsworthy I might have said to hell with it — let's be happy. But as things are, I can't put my own needs first.'

Andrea's stomach turned over. 'What about my needs?'

He sat back, his face suddenly inscrutable. 'What are they Andy? If I asked you to leave the theatre — what then?'

I love you, she wanted to say; nothing else matters.

As the silence lengthened his eyes narrowed and he said dully, 'You see. There really is only one answer.'

She turned away. 'If you really wanted me . . . '

His breathing was suddenly ragged, his voice sore. 'I want you. My God, don't ever think I don't want you.'

Dying leaves swirled between their feet and danced across the abandoned bandstand as the first raindrops started to fall.

Andrea shivered. 'This,' she said, 'must be the shortest love affair ever.'

He nodded bleakly. He understood, and had known what her answer would be.

During the short walk to the park gates she felt deathly calm.

'Tell me,' she said, when they reached his car. 'Why did you want me so much, at the beginning?'

'I was obsessed, my love,' he answered bitterly. 'I knew that with my guidance you could go far. Let's say that I had a dream, and now the dream is over. But for you, it's just beginning. You don't need me now, your goal is in sight.'

He pulled a handkerchief from his pocket and ran it beneath her eyes. 'No — it's nothing to cry about. Stick to your dream — and be happy.'

Something died in her as she watched him drive away and, desperate to reach somewhere where she and her misery could hide, stumbled across the common.

She let herself into the building, making a wet trail across the tiles in the hall that seemed a strange hall.

Does love always do this, she wondered bitterly, hearing the squelch of her shoes as she ran up the stairs. Make you change from self sufficiency to dependence, and turn the world outside empty and desolate when he goes. If so, wasn't it taking an awful chance to love?

When she closed the door behind her, she found, instead of the home she had left an hour before, a place where she had never been.

'God, the world has changed since yesterday, as if I've moved to a different planet,' she cried, in exasperation, letting the damp skirt slither to the floor.

She ripped off the jacket. Stop this Andrea. Your mind is going over and over everything like an express train. You're not a bloody psychiatrist.

Oh no! She clapped her hand to her forehead. The appointment with Don. Mortified, she ran to the telephone. There was no way she could keep her date with the psychiatrist. Her mind was too bruised and sore to allow anyone to probe there today.

Her biggest test now was the evening performance. The show must go on. And to prove it she started, in a shaky voice, to sing her songs.

9

When Andrea allowed herself time to think, she admitted that the following weeks were the hardest of her life. Only on stage was she happy. Only in her work could she lose herself and avoid pain.

The worst part was behaving normally with Gabriel, and she wondered that while nothing really intimate had occurred between them, they had irretrievably mislaid the people they were.

He no longer baited her; on the surface they got on better than before, yet perversely she yearned for the old days when he would shout and yell and she would retaliate. There was a distressing gentleness between them now, benevolent, even fatherly on his side, and she began to wonder if she had dreamed that Sunday afternoon, until he called into her dressing-room before the show one evening.

'There's an audition at The Royal for an American style extravaganza,' he said tersely. Only a faint softening of his bullet like words and a flickering in his cheek betrayed emotion.

Andrea twisted on the stool, watching him as he lounged, with arms folded, against the wardrobe.

'I can't fix it for you,' he warned.

Her eyes lingered greedily over his face, discovering darker shadows, deeper hollows and sharper curves.

He seemed unable to break away from her gaze, and his eyes flickered warily. 'I assume you still wish to leave?'

She clasped her hands together in her lap until the knuckles turned white. 'You're obviously doing your best to get rid of me as quickly as possible.'

Immature, spiteful words, she knew, and immediately wished she could withdraw them. Obviously, making a pass at her that day had meant nothing to him he probably regretted it and found her an embarrassment, thus his attempt to help her on her way.

His arms dropped to his sides and he shook his head, perching on the chair arm. 'Andy, Andy, I'm trying to help both of us, but you most of all. I let you down, my darling. I wasn't free to love you. I'm older than you, should know better, and I was in a position of trust. Your father . . . '

Andrea frowned. 'What about Dad?'

He studied his nails. 'Before your parents left they came to see the show, remember? Your father took me aside and,' Gabriel gave a bitter laugh, 'sort of warned me off.'

She jumped to her feet. 'He had no right. I'm not a child.'

'I told him I saw you as such,' Gabriel replied. 'I promised to keep an eye on you.'

He leaned forward and took her hands in his. 'You must see that we can't continue working together darling.'

She bit her lip, aware of his touch

leaping up her arms like sparks from a fire, and her heart pounding with miserable joy.

'The fact that I love you,' he went on, 'doesn't give me the right to mess up your life and career. Your career is the most important thing to you, isn't it?' His eyes bored into hers like blue shafts.

Her head whirled. Damn the effect he had on her! She couldn't think straight. Dragging her hands free she turned and sat down with her back to him, her mind in a turmoil. She could still change her mind, is that what he meant? Or was he trying to let her down lightly? Why did he have to be so old-fashioned? Many people had affairs today. She was startled by waves of hatred, despising what she saw as weakness. If he really wanted me . . . most people I know grab what they want from life, she scorned, disbelieving his unselfishness, the existence of self-sacrifice and reading both as uncaring.

She was staring into the mirror and

in the centre of the blazing bulb-edged frame she suddenly saw his face, watching her. Recognizing, she knew, the scorn and disbelief there.

The muscle twitched in his cheek, and his shoulders sagged. Without a word, he slowly stood up, turned towards the door and paused with his hand on the knob. There seemed to be an extraordinary long silence.

'To continue what I came to say,' he said sadly, 'I can't fix anything. Harold will choose the person he thinks is right for the part. He has to. But you'll have an advantage.'

'Oh?' Despite herself Andrea felt curious.

'Remember that Charity Ball we did in March?'

She nodded.

'Harold was there and has therefore heard you sing — he liked what he heard. Good luck.'

There was his old bitter smile. 'I made you do that old number, the one you labelled — I believe — sickly, yucky. It's the sort of number he'll be putting in his show.'

The door snapped shut, leaving Andrea with a heaviness in the pit of her stomach as she contemplated life without him — and how soon she was due on stage and, which song was it she had sung at the ball?

★ ★ ★

The man who looked like a cross between a gnome and an eagle, handed Andrea a sheet of music, asking in a hoarse voice, 'Sing this one for me darling?'

She raised her eyebrows. 'That's an oldie.'

He nodded, his bottom lip protruding. 'That's it. Nostalgia. It's what they want. The public is ready to return to melody.'

Andrea nodded. 'Gabriel thought the same. I know this number.' She tossed the song sheet on top of the piano and nodded at the pianist.

All her heart went into that soulful love song. 'Melancholy Out Of A Song' was its title, and melancholy she felt indeed, as she sang the warm low notes which one critic had said reminded him of sipping hot, creamy chocolate in front of a fire full of dreams.

At the end of the song Harold nodded. 'You'll do. You have the voice for it darling.'

Then he added curiously, 'Gabriel mentioned you started with a pop group. Seems hard to believe, with a voice like yours — it's so deep and mellow.' He patted the chair beside him. 'Sit down and tell me your story. Shirley,' he nodded at the pianist. 'Take a break now, darling.'

Andrea perched on the chair and told him her life story. '. . . then we reached the finals in a television talent contest.' Her voice thickened at the memory. 'We came second. Gabriel was one of the judges.'

She used his name with bitter sweet pleasure. 'Gabriel needed a singer and asked me to join him.'

Harold dropped his cigar butt on to the stage and ground it with the heel of his shoe. 'You left the boys?'

Her heart was heavy enough, without being made to feel guilt, she thought, touched by the anger that came so easily these days. 'Of course,' she snapped.

'And the boyfriend?'

'I haven't seen him . . . any of them . . . for a year now.' Andrea fought to control her impatience. 'We weren't serious anyway, Spike and I. He was my first boyfriend that's all.'

'The theatre though, is serious, isn't it darling?'

There was kindness in his gravelly voice, and Andrea gave a tremulous grin. 'It's my life.'

'I know a dedicated performer when I see one.' Standing up he was hardly any taller than Andrea herself, yet her hand was squashed inside his giant palm.

'I'll be in touch about the contract,'

he promised, as she freed herself.

'By the way darling,' he called as she walked away, 'my regards to Gabriel. Tell him he's the loser.' His hoarse chuckle followed her into the shadow of the wings.

★ ★ ★

They gave a party for her on the last night, squeezing into Gabriel's dressing-room because it was the largest and held a piano.

She thought of the first night and the party at the nightclub. And afterwards, Gabriel took her home.

As if she had called him, he came pushing towards her, head and shoulders above everyone else.

With a final thrust he reached her side. 'Tired?'

He always knows, she thought.

He slipped the empty glass from her listless hand and passed her another. The noise around them faded and his eyes, meeting hers, asked a question.

Yes, her own eyes replied. I do wish I was staying. I don't want to go. I'm frightened.

She smiled, raising her glass. 'Good luck to Sylvana, your new girl.' The words she had wanted to sound generous, came out like splintered glass.

'Remember everything I've taught you,' he pressed. 'Don't forget, when you walk on stage, you can only see the first ten rows so fix your mind on one person there and sing to that person; think of his hopes and dreams, his problems.'

'How can I forget what you taught me.' She gulped down the drink. 'You — the proverbial slave driver.'

Someone jostled her from behind and she tottered. Gabriel immediately reached out and drew her close. Whenever I smell sandalwood, she thought, I shall feel these arms holding me like the walls of home. What a strange feeling — out of all the men in the world, these are the only arms I want to be wrapped in. How can it be? Where does it come from, this magic? She tipped back her head to search his eyes, so that he caught his breath at the question there, and the pleading.

Emotion swirled around them, touching nerve ends already tautly stretched from weeks of reaching out like vines, unable to find a hold. Instinctively he moved so that they were scarcely touching, yet every inch of their bodies seemed welded together, as nerves met — touched — sizzled. She saw perspiration in tiny beads on his upper lip. He saw the darkening and expanding of her pupils and a pulse beating in the base of her throat.

Just this once, her eyes pleaded. I can't go away without knowing you really love me.

Will you hate me if I do, or hate me if I don't, his eyes sadly replied? I couldn't bear you to go hating me.

She lowered her head and spoke against the handkerchief that peeped from his jacket pocket; he had to bend to hear her voice. 'I'm not a child Gabby. I'm a woman.'

'Get your coat darling. I'm taking you home.'

Andrea said her goodbyes as they gathered around to wish her luck. But at last, loaded with flowers, she escaped to the car-park. She waited in her car until he had settled himself in his own, then followed him out into the street, hating the cold night air that deodorized the emotional haze she was under; wishing with all her might that she had no car with her that night. She could have been curled up in the seat beside Gabriel.

She followed him through London backways, past Big Ben, like a traffic policeman with hands at 1.15 and across Westminster Bridge.

Heading towards the Old Kent Road she knew she would always remember this. Her remoteness in the darkened car, the dim, deserted territory passing outside, the intensity of her concentration on his solid presence in front and the magnetic pull of those twin red lights, the motion of the car and the sickly sweet scent of a hundred petals.

Gabriel was already parked in the kerb when she drew up. He locked his car door, walked to meet her, and they went inside without touching. She had the key ready to open the door and shut it silently behind them. They stood together in the dark, and despite her dislike of the dark, she wanted it that way. She wanted to touch him, to remember the feel and the fragrance of him without distraction. Gabriel too, seemed to want to hide in darkness.

Andrea felt like a feather when he effortlessly picked her up and carried her into the bedroom. He placed her on the bed and went to the window, whisking the curtains closed on the face of the clock — her usual companion through the dark night.

Hearing the rustle of his starched shirt she felt suddenly unsure — about so many things — the thinness of her body. Should she undress? Her heart thumped and she was trembling violently. Until he came to her and drew the clothes from her body, gently turning her on to her side to pull down a zip, fumbling with her bra and panties. All the time murmuring words of love and reassurance.

'You're beautiful darling . . . I've waited so long . . . '

'I love you Gabby.' Strange that she wanted to cry.

'I know you do darling.'

Why did his voice sound so sad? She felt a shock when his fingers touched bare flesh on her thighs and slowly inched her flimsy tights down each leg; heat radiated from his body — she heard his breathing quicken and the loudness of his heartbeat.

She trembled as early morning air touched her skin and he paused, sending a surge of impatience through her so that she kicked away the remaining piece of nylon. Her body leapt to meet his, but he held her away, caressing her skin with light fingertips and burning lips until she almost screamed in exasperation. She grasped at him, her senses reeling. It was then he allowed his body to sink down on to hers until she felt her narrow body covered from head to toe, satisfying, and weightless.

Her hands crept to his broad back and surprised at the velvety feel of his skin she stroked exploratory fingers up and down and across his shoulders, over the hill of his buttocks, up the curve of his waist, lightly running the tips of her fingers down his spine. When he squirmed, she felt a wave of exultation and he groaned, burying his face in her hair, rocking to and fro gently — until her rhythm matched his own. Then he allowed fire to consume them both until they writhed in waves of delirium and pain was running in a glorious line from her navel, plunging down her body like a burning fuse — until at last — between her thighs — a magnificent explosion.

10

'Umbrellas?' Andrea threw all the scorn she could muster into the word. Hands on hips, she stood at the front of the stage glaring down at Harold. 'Am I right in thinking I'll be dressed in a plastic mac?'

Harold's big, shaggy head was sunk into his shoulders; he scribbled in a notebook. 'That's right.'

'I thought this show was supposed to be about glamour. Some glamour! Dressed in plastic macs from Woolworths.' She marched to the back of the stage.

'Andrea darling.'

She turned. He was crossing the boards towards her.

'Andrea darling, your job is to sing, mine is to picture what the stage will look like as you walk down the stairs while the girls, also in macs and carrying umbrellas, sing the chorus.' He took a breath. 'The song, after all, is about rain.'

She shrugged. The piano began to play the opening bars of the song.

'Let me explain.' He grasped her arm. And ignoring her deep sigh he asked gently, 'Have you read any Somerset Maugham?'

'No.'

'The show is loosely based upon his story *Rain*, about a love affair in the tropics. It starts in England and moves to a tropical island. Believe me — in this story there's a lot of rain.'

He grinned and chucked her under the chin. Her lips twitched and with a surge of affection she watched him amble from the stage, thump down the steps and settle himself in the front row of the stalls.

She took up her position; the resigned pianist started again.

Her voice rose — emotional, sensual, a little husky and breathless, drifting with the tide of guitar and piano. The tempo increased, the mood intensified, until the stage lights were cut, leaving her alone in the spotlight, face contorted with anguish and ecstasy as she moaned responses to the guitar.

'What difference will tomorrow make — another yesterday without love . . . and rain, rain, rain.'

The lights went on again. 'Perfect, pet. Now if I can get Cliff's song right, and the chorus manages to get together on the railway station number, we might . . . just might . . . make the opening next week.'

★ ★ ★

Andrea pushed open the door of the cloakroom, hit by a wall of scent and chatter. A big, blonde girl with a bulbous, swarthy face that was surprisingly attractive, detached herself from the rest. 'Hi Andrea, you look all in,' she said kindly.

'I am,' Andrea replied with fervour.

'Going out with handsome escorts

every night is tiring.' The other girl gave a knowing wink.

Andrea clicked her tongue. 'Meredith, what is it about me that makes people assume I lead a glamorous life with men clambering on to the stage fighting to take me out? If you must know I always go home and eat alone.' She took her coat and handbag from the wardrobe.

Meredith watched Andrea struggle into the coat. 'I suppose it's because you seem to have done so well for yourself, so quickly.'

'And no one can imagine I've done it myself; I have to have a dozen sugar daddies, I suppose,' Andrea flashed. 'It makes me so mad. If I were a man it would be put down to talent and hard work, but because I'm a woman . . . ' Shaking her head impatiently she moved towards the door.

Meredith reached out and held her back. 'Look. Come to dinner with us tonight.'

Andrea hesitated, thinking of her

lonely flat or a table for one at Mario's. At last her mouth curled into a tight smile. 'Thanks for asking, I'd like that.'

She drove to the nightclub wondering what she had let herself in for. In the eight weeks since she had left Gabriel she had thrown herself whole-heartedly into rehearsals, determined to do well and make Gabriel proud of her. And, she had to admit, hoping he would wish he hadn't lost her. When she wasn't rehearsing at the theatre, she was practising her songs at home, standing at the window singing to the white-faced clock.

In masochistic moments she strolled to the park and sipped tea in the tea rooms, well wrapped up against the frost. Sundays were still lost days. She did her chores, wrote to her parents and sometimes stared out of the window at the road that wound into Kent.

The memory of the morning she had awoken to find him gone still rankled. Some time during the night she had nestled close to him, smiling to herself in the dark when she found herself on the edge of the single bed as his big body took most of the space. She had curled herself around him, feeling sure that after this he wouldn't be able to leave her and would work something out. Secure and contented, she had drifted back to sleep.

In the morning he was gone.

The one night had left indelible fingerprints on her body and her heart. Invisible to others, they clung to her and refused to be shaken off. That, plus her burning ambition kept her aloof from other men, wrapped up in daydreams and hard work, and in her heart and her manner — already spoken for. She hurried off after rehearsals, seldom dawdling to gossip, as if she had somewhere to go. Emotionally she had shut herself off from men, and she supposed she couldn't blame them for taking themselves and their pride off in search of more flattering companions.

Now, bemused, she found herself in

the midst of a crowd. A large table in the centre of the restaurant held the ebullient group comfortably and while she let much of the banter slip over her, she found it quite pleasant to eat, drink wine and join in with laughter.

Meredith gave a sudden shout of recognition. 'There's Simon. Pull up another chair Andrea, Simon's here.'

'Hello Simon,' Andrea murmured.

His blue-black eyes threw a look of impish charm from one girl to the other, 'I've been looking forward to meeting you Andrea. This is my lucky night.'

'Oh?'

'I've heard a lot about the new star of *Storm*.'

'You've heard wrong then; I'm not the star at all.'

'Then you should be.' His voice was serious and Andrea was uncomfortably aware that he still held her hand and there was a steely glint in Meredith's eyes.

She pulled her hand away and turned

towards the girl on her other side. 'What was your last show Janice?'

Listening to Janice with only half an ear, she heard Meredith and Simon chatting together and joking with the people around them. He seemed to know them all well.

Later, she tossed and turned in bed, her mind too active to settle. She was, she realized, stimulated by the evening. Recently she had hidden herself away, apart from rehearsals, hoping for the telephone to ring, even going to the tea rooms in the park and expecting to see Gabriel there sitting at the table beneath the trees, throwing crumbs to the birds.

She had been living in too small a circle and her mind had atrophied so that she'd lost herself in sleep. Now, with conversation and laughter, she had come alive, able to think with scorn of the little mouse scuttling to her room every night to brood.

What a good thing she had gone out with the crowd tonight. It had pulled her to her senses, taken her out of a rut. She needed stimulation. Otherwise she would soon have found herself singing like an automaton without feelings or emotions. She could have ruined her career with self-pity.

So what, that she had lost the man she loved — her parents too. There was a whole world out there, full of people. What was she doing hiding here for goodness sake? This was no way for a star to behave. Think positive.

You've been a fool, Andrea. Start living again.

★   ★   ★

Andrea stared at her reflection in the mirror. Behind her, dingy whitewashed walls trickled with condensation. It was hard to imagine that beyond the dirty high up window lay the glittering West End, for she was isolated by anxiety and adrift from the world, it seemed.

The girls were now on stage for the first number. Particles of powder and

145

remnants of fear floated in the air, settling on dressing-tables, mirrors and hastily flung down coats. Fluffy powder puffs crowded with hair brushes, combs, and stained tissues; make-up brushes had been flung down among bottles, tubes, irons and tongs.

Andrea drew in deep lungfuls of breath until her heart quietened. Out loud, she repeated Gabriel's words. 'Try to free your mind from any anxiety about results.'

A sharp rap on the door started her heart racing again. 'Come in.'

A grinning face came around the door followed by a giant bouquet of roses and carnations. How strange, she thought, I was just thinking of Gabriel.

'Thanks Jimmy,' she smiled, opening her arms.

The cellophane crackled when she ripped it open and searched for the card. The small, neat writing said: *Good luck. Can I take you out to dinner after the show to celebrate the birth of a star? Simon.*

Andrea laid the bouquet down. Her skin prickled and a damp coating of fear gathered on her legs and in the palms of her hands. Disappointment? Or fear at the challenge in Simon's note?

'Five minutes Miss Grace.'

She jumped up. Shivering at the touch of the plastic mac she thrust her feet into little white boots, picked up a frilly umbrella and hurried from the room. Very faintly along the corridor echoed the girls' voices sweeping into the final bars of their song.

Entering from back stage Andrea recognized none of the other girls as she wandered through their ranks; they were just pretty girls in colourful plastic macs. Some sat and others lounged against pillars, a refreshment stall or a ticket office.

Automatically the words came: 'What difference will tomorrow make, now my lover has gone . . . ' But to her ears her voice sounded weak, until she reached front stage and through a gap in the chorus line she saw the audience. Specks of golden dust scurried up the spot-light to the roof, and her nostrils caught the heavy cloud of perfume and the smell of hot lights.

When her voice rose to its full power she sensed a reaction from the audience and looked down to the first ten rows, singing to them, coaxing even more emotion into the melody.

She aimed her voice towards the furthest ones, the invisible people, gathering a little bit from each one and bringing it back to pour into herself. Gabriel had told her to think about individuals out there. They had worries, he used to say. They were bored, tired, expectant, sad. Perhaps had been through a hard day.

Her voice flew towards them like a lasso — then she tugged gently on their emotions and pulled them towards her.

She breathed the last low note into the microphone — heard a burst of applause — and immediately turned and walked off-stage. Then she was in the wings with people crowded around her, surprised to see them there — because she had forgotten them.

Harold grasped her arm. 'Great darling. Wonderful.'

Flashing him a smile she joined the other girls in the stampede along the corridor towards the dressing-room to change for the second half.

★   ★   ★

On bare feet, the girls milled around on stage against a backdrop of dark green jungle. They wore pieces of colourful cloth across one shoulder and down to their knees. As Andrea passed between them they formed themselves into neat lines, swaying and waving their arms.

Composed, but brittle, she reached centre stage, and paused before sauntering towards the footlights. There, she stood alone, the white low-necked dress clinging to her thighs, candescent in the spotlight. Surprised, she heard recognition applause and beneath the wide-brimmed hat her smile grew wide and she caught her breath with delight, so she was slightly late with her opening. But the slip was barely noticeable and she made up for it by singing for all she was worth.

Flushed with joy, nerves calm, she hated every moment she was off-stage. For the last number she sang a duet with Cliff, the lead singer, until the chorus gathered for the finale. With a shock, she realized it was all over.

She stood with the chorus as they took their bows, then Cliff stepped back from his place in the front, took her hand and pulled her out of line to take a bow with him. The audience went wild, the rumble turning to a roar, interspersed with whistles and shouts.

Then the curtain fell for the last time. The roar faded. It was as if Andrea's lifeline was cut. There was movement swirling all around her; she was caught up in hugs and kisses from people she didn't know.

Harold pushed through the crowd,

pulled a cigar from his mouth and kissed her on both cheeks. 'I knew I was right about you,' he chortled. Turning around he waved an arm. 'You were all great. Party's at my place.'

Outside she found Cliff busy signing autographs and immediately hands came forward to Andrea, holding books, scraps of paper and pro-grammes. The theatre door closed, the world shifted, like a kaleidoscope. There were pale faces, thrusting hands, pens and paper; winking neon signs; car horns, squealing brakes. A cold, slip-pery blackness above.

Pulling her coat tightly around her she searched the faces of the crowd, for some reason thinking of her parents. The step beneath her feet was worn and uneven; above her head the illuminated sign carried the magic words — Stage Door.

Then she was in a car that hesitantly parted streams of people spilling into the road from the crowded pavement. Wind tossed the hair and skirts of passing women — Andrea snuggled back against soft leather and closed her eyes.

Ten minutes later they swooped into Harold's apartment. A stranger there, Andrea wandered hesitantly into the great lounge overlooking the Thames; chatter and laughter rose and fell in waves, accompanied by the tinkling notes of a grand piano. She walked towards a marble mantelpiece, fascinated by a great mirror in a carved gilt frame. With a movement of the crowd she saw the pianist reflected in the glass. He saw her at the same time, immediately stopped playing and walked towards her, taking her hands in his.

'I've written a song for you.'

'What is it called?'

' 'My Star' ,' said Simon.

11

Later, when the party was at its
height, he came to find her, edging his
way through the crowd, slim and
ethereal-looking, with flared nostrils, a
determined chin and those dark eyes.
Last time she glimpsed him he was
talking to Meredith, standing an inch
shorter than the girl who glowered
down at him.

They met in the middle of the room.
'Feel like dinner darling?' he asked.

'I'm much too excited to eat.'

His next words brought the blood
rushing to her already heated cheeks.
'You need someone to look after you
my darling.'

She choked back a wave of irritation.
Why did men always want to manage
and dominate her? Her father, Gabby,
now Simon.

'Hey,' he laughed. 'Why the ferocious

look? Women don't usually react that way when I make suggestions.' His mouth curved, giving him such an angelic expression she had to smile. Whereupon he removed the glass from her hand, lightly grasped her shoulder and nudged her forward.

'Let's get out of this crush. Seriously, my love, you've probably had little to eat today because of nerves and now you're full of drink. Never drink on an empty stomach. While we eat we can discuss something.'

Andrea frowned, twisting around to search the crowd.

'It's all right,' he added. 'I told Harold I was taking you to dinner and said we'll be back in time for the papers.'

'Honestly!' she said crossly, yet her lips twitched. He probably thought she'd had too much to drink and could persuade her into some shady business deal. She was, in fact, completely sober. She was also her father's daughter.

Drawing herself up, she shook his

hand off her shoulder. 'I can manage thank you.'

And made her way unsteadily to the door.

★ ★ ★

The restaurant was almost deserted — shutting London out with the click of the door. Dim table lamps flickered beneath low beams and a log fire threw out welcoming gusts of heat. There was even a cat asleep on a stool before the fire, and surrounded by portraits of Dickensian characters and rich red decor, she started to relax.

'I'll order for you darling,' he suggested as the waiter appeared.

Her chin went up. 'I'll choose my own thank you.'

Taking her time she chose scampi and chips with strawberry cheesecake to follow.

'Hungry?' he asked.

'Famished!'

He filled their glasses from a bottle of

sparkling wine. 'See, I'm good for you.'

He ate his omelette and salad neatly and with little enthusiasm while they talked about *Storm*, and he questioned her about her life.

'That's enough of me,' she said at last. 'What do you actually do?' She was a guest, being taken out by a stranger when there was someone else she would rather be with. She had a sweeping sense of *déjà vu*. There had been another time, such as this . . . she must act her part . . .

He leaned back in his chair. 'I had no talent unfortunately to tread the boards; by sheer hard work though, and a certain . . . ' he paused, 'a certain sensitivity, combined with a romantic nature, I found I could write songs.'

His voice was low and intense. 'Haven't done too badly. I wrote *Cloudburst*. Did you know that writers' royalties on record sales are higher than the performer? There are royalties on sheet music as well, you see. And every time a song is played the composer benefits. Lennon and McCartney earn more from writing than performing.'

He glanced at her expectantly, and she nodded. 'I like *Cloudburst*.'

'So many groups and soloists write their own material now,' he sighed, 'that for the songwriter it's very much a question of the right song in the right place at the right time. The best way is to pick an artist and submit a song to their agent.'

He paused while the waiter cleared the table and handed him the bill on a plate.

'Last year I decided it was time to put to good use all my experience in show business and go into management. So I set up as an agent. I have a few people on my books but I'm hardly a Lew or Leslie Grade yet. What I need,' he smiled, 'is someone big. A star.'

He beckoned to the waiter.

'As soon as I heard you sing darling, I knew you were right for me — that we would make good music together.

You're star material.'

Andrea felt suddenly dejected. The word material echoed in her mind. It's like being a lump of clay, she thought, there's always someone waiting to shape me into their own design. Her skin prickled with tired nerve ends and she heard another voice, not so long ago, using almost the same words.

'You need someone to take care of the business side of things,' Simon was saying.

A sudden yawn threatened to split her face apart.

He laughed. 'See. Even the mention of business makes you yawn.'

She nodded. 'I must agree with you there.'

With no hint of tiredness, he enthused, 'I'll fight to get the best possible return for your talent. What kind of contract do you have with Harold?'

Her heart lurched as she remembered the last time she was with Gabriel and he went over Harold's contract with her, giving it his approval, before she left him. That had been just before the party. Her mind grew muzzy. And after the party . . .

Simon wiped his mouth on his napkin and stood up. 'What do you say? Shall we give it a try?' His voice, though light, was threaded with steel. 'You need me, you know, as much as I need you.'

Shaken to find herself, tonight of all nights, plunging into depression, she nodded.

He helped her on with her coat and stood with both hands on her shoulders; their eyes were level. 'That's a deal Andrea. Now let's get back.'

★   ★   ★

Andrea sat in front of the picture window overlooking the Thames. There had been no need to ask about the reviews when they arrived; the sound of singing and cheering met them as they stepped out of the lift.

Startled, she heard a cheer go up when they walked through the door; soon she was being hugged, kissed and congratulated. A glass was thrust into her hands, and a cascade of champagne spurted into it, surging over the rim and drenching her hands and skirt. She laughed. Because it was, after all, a night for laughing. She had known the audience liked her; but if the critics liked the whole show, they were set for a long run.

Simon's eyes shone. 'You've made it darling. They all mention you — the offers will come rolling in now, you wait and see. Read this!'

She laughed. 'Cold black and white words. It's the applause that told me Simon. I don't read papers.'

He threw down one newspaper and picked up another. 'One wise guy mentioned Gabriel Fox.'

A shawl of cold air passed through the window, settling around her shoulders. The newspaper hid his face and she could see only his long slender fingers as he read aloud: 'Gabriel Fox's audiences are finding that without His Grace the show is a little dull, and I hear that when it closes Graceless Fox will return to the ballroom. There is no doubt he is the Prince of the Ballrooms.'

He dropped the paper in her lap. 'Back in a sec.' She watched him speed across the room and speak urgently to Harold. The noise faded away. She was reliving the tours: Sundays spent travelling; packing and unpacking; grumpy landladies, dressing-rooms like cupboards, dirty windows and dingy lino, the piers, the Winter Gardens, the town halls, the Policemen's Balls; the decreasing number of ballrooms, as they closed to make way for bingo or supermarkets.

A reflection in the window cut across her memories and she turned sharply.

'Congratulations,' drawled Meredith, waving an empty glass and swaying to and fro.

'Thank you . . . ' Andrea began.

'Done well for yourself,' the girl continued. 'Do they know how you use them?'

Andrea frowned. 'I don't know what . . .'

'You dropped Gabriel Fox when it suited you — now you have Simon.' She turned away. 'Congrats,' she threw over her shoulder.

Andrea pressed her burning forehead to the cool glass. She was unlucky, it seemed, with women friends. No wonder she had preferred boys' company as a child; preferring to climb trees and play cricket rather than play with girls. But, she brought her thoughts back to the present, why should she let Meredith spoil her night anyway . . . to hell with her!

Fearful of the nostalgia that threatened to dilute her new-found success, she sharply suggested to Simon when he returned that they discuss the contract.

He pointed out that she would have nothing to think about except her voice and appearance. Everything else would be left to him. Ten per cent of her earnings was a small price to pay for such a service.

'A complete management package darling. Extra services for people who sign with me, press agent, travel agent, secretarial help.' Reaching out, he covered one of her hands with his. 'The lot.'

Andrea snatched her hand away and reached out for the newspaper which lay open between them. The songs, she read, had a forties' post-war sadness, fifties' glamour, late fifties' unreality and seventies' reality. Andrea Grace, a talented newcomer to the musical, has a voice which plays on the heart strings like a harp. It vibrates there and somehow leaves an echo. Don't miss her . . .

'Well,' he asked urgently. 'What do you say?'

She had a sudden, frightening sensation of falling away from herself; a stranger sat there in her place; who was this stranger? Where was she going?

She stared at her reflection in the window. Light started to stain the sky as the curtain of night folded back to reveal another day — opening on a new world for Andrea.

The first thing Simon organized was a dressing-room of her own and a rise in salary. Disgusting — he called her room, and persuaded the manager to install a shower and toilet, and redecorate. He ensured she ate a snack of soup and fruit before she started to dress and make-up, and after each performance he took her out to dinner where he excitedly told her about the offers she had received.

'So far,' he counted on his fingers, 'a television guest appearance, a radio interview and hints of another musical next year.'

Andrea rarely read newspapers, but Simon delighted in reading out the more scandalous items concerning them. Sometimes he embroidered them until she snatched the paper away to see for herself. She was unworried by the publicity. 'It's fortunate Dad lives on the other side of the world,' she giggled, when Simon read that she was pregnant. 'I would have been rushing down to Kent today to explain it was only a stomach bug.'

★　★　★

'What difference will tomorrow make?' It was easy for Andrea to feel the pain of a girl whose lover has gone leaving her to faceless tomorrows; made sure the audience felt it too as she weaved and threw around them a delicate cobweb of haunting sadness.

Thursday matinées, rarely a full house, held a different audience, more difficult to hold, as if they were denied the magic that night time brings, and unready for dreams because daylight lingered outside waiting to snatch them back into a winter afternoon.

By the end of the first half the

atmosphere changed, with less fidgeting, more applause. The quietness that settled over the audience when she sang her solos signalled that she carried them with her.

After each performance, Harold's face was the first thing her eyes sought; he either beamed with his face shiny like the moon, or his face grew long and he tugged at his beard. He became her barometer.

Today he was shining. He took her coat from a chair and tucked it around her as she trooped off stage surrounded by chorus girls, with Cliff following.

She felt a tug on the empty dangling sleeve of the coat, and Cliff squeezed past. 'Great show darling. See you later.' She watched him speed down the corridor towards his dressing-room.

People milled around, high spirited with relief. There were shrieks of laughter, excited chatter, shoes pounding on the iron staircase leading to the upstairs dressing-rooms, much shouting and crashing of doors.

Beyond the safety curtain members of the orchestra would be packing away their instruments and disappearing beneath the stage; stragglers from the audience would be pushing through exit doors leaving the great auditorium empty and silent with upturned red plush seats standing ignominiously and ingloriously in a sea of litter.

'Simon coming later?' asked Harold.

Andrea nodded, leaning forward to kiss his squat face. 'I'll rest, perhaps read, and wait for Simon to bring the soup.'

She closed the door with a sigh of relief. Her dressing-room was now the haven it was supposed to be — thanks to Simon. Warm, comfortable, quiet, full of her favourite things; her records and books and always, always overflowing with flowers and good luck cards. But the card she longed for was never there.

Bulbs around the mirror shone down on to pots, brushes, a framed photograph of her suntanned parents, tissues and scent. In a layer of powder stood a blue and yellow earthenware pitcher filled with bronze chrysanthemums and at it feet — a blue envelope.

Andrea picked it up curiously. Not air mail. A fan? Expensive, thick paper. Sinking on to the stool she studied the large writing in blue-black ink before she tore open the envelope.

She stared down at the name scrawled across the single sheet of blue notepaper. Her heart began to thump painfully. He had never written to her before, but she recalled seeing his signature many times. It was as she remembered, with the big loop on the G and L.

12

His name jumped from the page and she was suddenly shaking. She checked the embossed address at the top right-hand side of the paper, murmuring softly to herself. 'Tanglewood.'

Dear Andrea. How cold, she thought. *I'm home from Germany earlier than expected and I must see you. Can you come here? It will be quite safe any afternoon this week.*

That was all. The blood rushed to her face. What could it possibly mean? Germany? She didn't even know he was in Germany. And the tone — as if all was not over between them. As if the months apart had never been. Her thoughts whirling, she struggled for an explanation, grappled with every possibility. Had he written before, asking for a reconciliation and the letter been lost in the post? That would explain the terse note. Obviously his wife wasn't there — why?

The notepaper trembled in her hand. It was a shock, yet, she realized, not completely unexpected. Hoped for. Yes, hoped for. With a flash of insight she knew that while she had been able to immerse herself in work, seeming to forget Gabby with the sheer necessity of concentrating and holding herself together for the show, deep down she had known she would see him again. Hadn't known when or how. She would meet him face to face in a crowded street; he would be sitting in her dressing-room when she came off-stage; he would phone; he would write. She had known it would happen one day, yet wouldn't admit even to herself, the longing.

Now she was swept with an overriding gladness, a sweet and powerful emotion that surged to rocket her to his side. There was no guilt, no sorrow, not even surprise any more. Just eagerness.

Without stopping to clean her face

she threw a coat over the white dress, grabbed a handbag and rushed to the door.

Muttering beneath her breath, she fought the rush-hour traffic that surged over Westminster Bridge. She would only have a short time with him as it was. What a fool she was to go all that way just for an hour. She could wait until tomorrow when there was no matinée.

She laughed out loud. How could she wait? And how could someone who had just discovered she was a weak-willed fool be filled with the most extraordinary lightness of spirit?

What's happened, she wondered? Why ask her to go to Tanglewood? Why didn't he just come to the theatre, or her flat? Perhaps because of Simon; the newspapers made much of the relationship. What had happened to his wife? Was she away having treatment again? Had they separated? Why was the note so mysterious?

She sped along the A2, thoughts

spinning with the wheels of the car. After what seemed a lifetime, she was turning into the lane.

Quickly she switched on the headlights, peering through the gloom at sign posts which would point her towards Tanglewood.

There was the pond! And behind the pub that queer little winding lane — the shops — the church.

And at long last — Tanglewood.

Surrounded by dusk blackened trees, the chalky cottage walls gave out an eerie glow, and she felt a familiar prickle running up and down her spine. Her feet were strangely lethargic on the garden path. He would, of course, be looking out for her. Any minute now the door would fly open . . .

Her hand curled around the lion's head knocker.

Twice the deep silence was splintered by an echoing crash, but there was no open door, no smiling Gabriel.

She rapped again, stepping back to inspect the upstairs windows, blank beneath their straw eyelids. Her hopes plummeted. Could she have made a fruitless journey?

Sick with disappointment she turned away, but stopped after a few steps, her mouth set in a stubborn line. She wasn't coming all this way for nothing, besides . . . she lifted her chin in the air . . . she sensed a mystery; something was wrong. He could be ill in there.

She trudged around the side of the house, through a gate set in a low wall on to a gravel path. Glancing up at the house she saw light coming from an upstairs window and a wave of relief quickly turned to concern. She was right he must be ill and couldn't get to the door. Hurriedly she tried a glass door. The handle turned smoothly beneath her hand. Stepping inside was like being hit in the face by a soggy woollen scarf — damp air was choked with the funereal scents of warm earth and chrysanthemums. Shuddering, she thrust her way through a miscellany of tools, plants, and wickerwork furniture.

At the other end of the room she came face to face with a heavy oak door. Slowly she turned the handle. The door creaked and swung open. Her footfall, as she crossed a square hall, was loud on flagstones.

'Hello Andrea.'

Andrea froze.

A woman was descending the stairs, clinging to the wrought-iron balustrade; the peach hem of her house-coat trailed behind.

'The door was open, I did knock . . . ' Andrea's shocked voice died away.

Like a doll — flashed into Andrea's mind when they stood face to face. Impeccably made-up, with her fawn hair neatly placed on top of her head, her round, childish eyes were like blue glass, her mouth a smiling crimson bow. Her nose was the sort that Andrea envied, inconspicuous, lying low with the hint of an uptip and swamped by her high curved forehead and full cheek-bones.

Her voice was low and crusty, almost ingratiating. 'I was expecting you. You see, I knew you would come.'

Andrea frowned. 'Gabriel asked me to come. Are you . . . ?'

There was another bright smile. 'I'm Jennifer Fox.'

Andrea's skin prickled. 'Where is Gabriel?'

'On the telephone dear. Upstairs in his room. I'll show you to his study; he wants you to wait there.'

With her head spinning Andrea climbed the stairs and passed a closed door. Suddenly her heart leapt. From the other half open door came Gabriel's voice.

Jennifer's plump fingers touched her arm. 'He hates being disturbed when he's talking business.'

Remembering Gabriel's tempers, Andrea allowed herself to be led up a narrow flight of stairs towards another landing with two doors. Jennifer opened the first door and stood aside, allowing Andrea to pass into a sloping floored room swamped by a massive old desk. Colourful rugs were scattered over the polished floor and bookshelves stood uncomfortably against bulging white-washed walls. There was a faint odour of tobacco.

'Take off your coat and sit down.' Jennifer indicated a chair in front of the desk. With a strangely sheepish smile, she scrabbled inside a drawer and brought out a key. 'Secrets,' she whispered, with a finger to her lips, and disappeared somewhere beneath the desk.

Troubled and vaguely embarrassed, Andrea turned and glanced at the door. If only Gabriel would hurry up.

With a crash a heavy book landed on the desk between them. Andrea jumped.

Jennifer's mood had completely changed. Gone was the simpering child, in her place was a hard-faced woman who leaned towards Andrea and slid the book across the desk. 'What do you think I found madam?'

Andrea was speechless.

'This.' Jennifer jabbed a bitten fingernail at the leather-bound book. 'A book all about you.' Breathing heavily she flung open the cardboard pages. 'He didn't tell me about you. Oh no. I had to search his desk to find out what was going on.'

Recoiling from the waft of gin, Andrea recalled the stumble on the stairs, the shaking hand on the balustrade. While on the desk her own face stared back at her in black and white newsprint. A picture of her with the group after the talent show; singing alone and with Cliff; coming out of the theatre. Reviews, and headlines too: *Crafty old Fox takes under his wing the beautiful rock and roll star Andrea Grace.*

She shook her head, dazed and taken aback by the venom that twisted the beautiful face before her.

Plump white hands turned the pages while Andrea sat stricken; wanting to stop them turning, yet instead, mesmerized, watching herself and Gabriel singing together, gazing into each other's eyes. *Is this for real*, quoted one headline. *The Fox and the Showgirl*, said another.

Andrea gulped and tore her eyes away. My goodness, when some of those pictures were taken they had hated the sight of each other.

'You know what they're like, the papers, they exaggerate. It's not what you think. I haven't seen him for months.'

'You're just like him, you think I'm a fool,' Jennifer rasped.

Andrea jumped to her feet.

Jennifer grasped her wrist. 'Look at you, dressed like the tramp you are — your face covered in muck.'

Struggling to push away those clinging fingers, Andrea was suddenly boiling with rage. 'Look here, this is . . . mad . . . let's go and see him. He'll tell you . . . '

Her words trailed away and she felt suddenly sick. 'Is that why he asked me to come here?' she whispered.

'To reassure *you*.'

Jennifer dropped Andrea's arm and stood up, moving swiftly to the door. 'I asked you to come.'

'Why should you do that?' Andrea asked curiously.

In reply the door slammed and Andrea was alone drenched in relief. She's going — Gabby will be in. A key scraped in the lock, and still she stood, until with a shrug she slowly crossed the room. 'How can the sophisticated Gabriel be married to anyone so childish?' she muttered, crossly.

It was when she reached the oak door and felt the round knob beneath her hands turn, and the door remain firmly shut, that annoyance turned to agitation.

She tugged and pounded on the door which although badly fitting, with a huge gap at the bottom, wouldn't budge.

'Gabby. Gabby. This is crazy. Open the door.' She rattled the handle, shook the door and kicked it, her voice rising to a shriek of fury as pain shot through her toes and up her legs.

It was useless. Fighting an urge to scream with frustration, she crossed the room towards the tiny window under the eaves and grappled with the lock until her fingers were raw and stained with rust. It was the scent of wood-smoke that finally brought helpless tears to her eyes — the scent of her childhood.

Angrily she brushed the tears away and turned to survey her prison. She sniffed again. And in the very same instant realized that it wasn't wood-smoke from outside. It was there — curling under the door — filling the room with unexpected and frightening speed.

Disbelief held her transfixed in the middle of the room. Through the gap at the bottom of the door came newspapers and rags — shiny liquid followed them in and ran in pools towards the rugs. The room stank of singed, scorched cloth; flames lapped at the puddles, pounced on the wool rugs and chewed at the polished wooden floor.

She grabbed her coat from the chair and beat at the flames — she heard a shout, but caught only one word. 'Justice.' The white fur was gobbled up in a trice by a tongue of fire.

With stinging eyes, raw throat and retching with the stench of paraffin she ran to the window and again tried to force the lock. Choking, she grasped a chair, swinging it at the window but to her despair it bounced off the small square panes. Next time she aimed just the leg of the chair at a single pane of glass, jabbing until it cracked. With grim determination she did the same to the others, and then pushed with all her might at the wooden frames.

Air. No longer behind glass, free for her use, and she took her fill of it. Cold, damp, honey-scented air, cooling her burning throat and lungs.

Hearing a roar she turned to see flames scaling the bookcase — reaching out across the sloping ceiling towards oak beams. For a few terrible moments she stood awestruck as the fire took on the form of a wild animal, devouring all in its path.

Moving backwards she slipped her head and shoulders through the window. Pain shot through her hands from jagged glass; blood trickled down her arms. Steeling herself, she wriggled backwards until she was sitting on the narrow ledge, gripping the window frame, terrified of looking down. There was raw, searing agony as glass shards pierced her thighs — there were clouds of pain filled darkness — and suddenly, a leaping wall of flame. Desperately she looked around. The tree was just too far to reach.

Pushing faintness away, she shakily stood up, grappling for a hold on rain-soaked thatch. Her blood-stained shoes hurtled to the ground.

Suddenly her foot slipped. 'No!' she screamed. She forced herself to freeze, with one leg dangling, giving herself time to recover; calming herself with deep painful breaths, until she felt able to turn around, painfully slowly, and grip the frame with her hands behind her. Heat scorched her stinging hands and legs and she knew there was only one exit.

Now, she screamed to herself. Now!

She leaped outwards, waiting in terror for the ground to rise up and crash into her.

The arms of the fat old oak tree reached out for her clawing hands. Bark ripped her skin as she scrabbled for a hold with her arms, legs and feet. Until at last, she nestled in its boughs, taking loud gasps of air.

This is a nightmare, it can't be real, it can't be! Unable to control her shaking body she saw the little window turn bright orange. Please God, let me wake up. But cold air on her smarting skin and agonizing pain from the cuts on her hands and legs, told her it was no nightmare. It was too horribly real.

Shock suddenly dammed her tears. Gabriel!

Ignoring the pain, she gingerly wriggled backwards, grasping branches and feeling for footholds. Her blood-streaked dress was ripped and she nearly lost her grip many times before her feet touched the ground. Then her arms were around the solid trunk, her head was pressed against the bark, and she was sobbing as if her heart would break.

A long time afterwards, when her tears were spent, she forced herself away from the tree. And then she was running, running with all her might towards the conservatory door which still stood ajar as she had left it.

In the hall she peered upwards. The flames hadn't yet reached the first landing.

Racing up the stairs two at a time she met swathes of thick blue-black smoke and made straight for the second door. She turned the knob and threw it open.

A masculine room. Single bed, chest

of drawers, wardrobe. Jennifer perched on the bed holding a tumbler, the bright smile on her face.

'Where's Gabriel?' Andrea screamed.

Running towards the bed she grasped Jennifer's shoulder, leaving bloody marks on the peach satin housecoat. The room stank of paraffin and gin and smoke.

Looking in despair around the room Andrea shook the woman again. 'Where is he?'

Jennifer laughed — a light, easy, young girl's laugh as she pointed at the chest of drawers — and a portable cassette player.

Then Andrea understood.

With tears streaming from her eyes, she pulled Jennifer's arm. 'Come on. Out.'

The tumbler fell to the carpet. Jennifer jerked back. Her eyes were protruding like blue marbles. 'I know what's been going on with you two. I made up my mind . . . the next time he's away I would get together with you. Then I read about you in the paper, and had a much better idea,' she gloated.

'Come ON,' Andrea gulped. 'The fire's coming.'

Somehow Andrea managed to drag the taller, heavier woman to the door.

'I know all about you,' the woman cried. 'You're having a baby. It's Gabriel's baby, isn't it?'

Andrea tore Jennifer's hands from the door. 'The papers lie. All the time. This way. Hurry.'

The woman swayed and would have fallen if Andrea hadn't thrown her own slim arms around her, taking her dead weight and dragging her towards the stairs.

But Jennifer was suddenly punching at Andrea in a bid to escape. Taken by surprise Andrea lost her grip, gasping as an elbow caught her in the chest. Then fingers were around her neck. She choked. Smoke swirled around her throat like a thick scarf — pulling tighter and tighter. Darkness and light came and went in waves.

The fingers fell away — Jennifer was doubled over, choking and retching and, taking her opportunity, Andrea threw both arms around her from behind, prepared, with the last of her strength, to push her down the stairs away from the flames that she could now see. She gritted her teeth. She had to save what belonged to him. To save what he cared for.

Unexpectedly Jennifer stood up, flinging out both arms, catching Andrea unawares and almost knocking her from her feet.

Andrea tightened her grip; she felt a blow in the small of her back — heard the crack of splintering wood. She opened her mouth to scream. But smoke muffled the sound that came from her throat and she fell backwards through silent space into darkness.

13

Andrea caught the tears before they fell; brushed them away and ran her hands across the dressing-table. She must have knocked the bag to the floor. She was bent down searching the carpet when the door opened.

'I'll get it Andy,' called Jane.

When the bag was pressed into her hands Andrea reached for the handkerchief.

'You look a right old mess,' Jane commented. 'Here.' Andrea felt the crisp touch of linen running beneath her eyes and down her cheeks.

'There,' said Jane. 'That's better.'

'Jane, I don't want to go back to the ballroom.'

'Right ho. Not much point anyway, you've been here ages. They were playing the last waltz when I left.'

Stiffly Andrea rose from the stool.

'Let's go home.'

Along the corridor, up narrow stairs, cold draught of air and footsteps ringing on a stone floor. Feeling of space. Then they were through the doors and descending steps to the street.

Fine rain pattered against her face and beat against her legs and she recalled just such a night when she sat in a car watching ordinary people wending their messy way home. She forgot where it was, or when, but it was strange to feel that, as if she was recalling a scene from a film seen a long time ago, that girl seemed like someone else now.

A hand fell on her shoulder, holding her back.

'Just a minute Andy. For God's sake — don't just walk away . . . '

She stopped dead. 'I must get home Gabby.'

'Wait,' he instructed, 'I'll get a cab.'

She heard the squeal of brakes and a cheerful voice. 'Where to mate?'

Then she was pulled forward and a gentle hand pressed her head down, making her bend to climb into the roomy, leathery taxi. Jane murmured their address and she was flung back into the seat as they jerked away from the kerb and joined the stream of traffic.

She was conscious of being trapped, of Gabby's warm thigh close to hers on one side and Jane's bony knee on the other; of the odour of damp clothes and sandalwood; of an urge to escape, even from dear Jane. Away from well meaning ministrations — and from the past which drifted over her like a lowering, stormy sky.

But she could only sit there between them, uncomfortable with the motion of the taxi as it stopped and started; fighting off panic, and memories which flew at her from the past like darts, coming thick and fast whether she allowed them or not.

To her own amazement, and that of the others, she suddenly laughed.

'What's funny?' asked Jane.

Andrea squeezed her friend's arm and turned her head the other way, towards the scent of sandalwood.

'I was thinking of the first time Gabby and I met. He kidnapped me that night too. Bullied me into getting into a cab with him — a stranger.'

Her voice faded. In the pulsing silence she felt their thoughts running neck to neck. Thoughts too deep and painful to voice. So much, because of that meeting, had happened. Tragedy. Lives changed. A life lost. If she hadn't gone with him that night, she would now have her sight — his wife would be alive.

She felt a wave of compassion. How he must be blaming himself, she realized. Impulsively she reached out, searching for his hand. When she found it he clutched hers almost desperately and, she sensed, with relief.

It was all she could do for him. Yet somehow she felt that it was enough.

'We're here,' called Jane brightly.

'Night Mr Fox.' The taxi driver cleared his throat. Andrea began to panic.

'Come on Andrea, you'll catch cold,' called Jane.

Andrea hesitated. 'Come in for a drink Gabby.'

His arm immediately went beneath her elbow. She heard the clink of coins, the slam of a car door, the splutter of engine. Then the tap tap of Jane's shoes across the pavement and Gabriel's heavy foot fall twice the length of her own uneven tread.

Once inside he busied himself helping the girls out of their coats. 'Where do I put these?' she heard him ask.

She sensed him prowling around the flat looking at the place she called home. The settee gave beneath his weight, bouncing her up and down. Jane crashed cups and saucers in the kitchen.

'We have a lot to talk about,' he was saying softly when Jane came into the room. He jumped up, took the tray and placed it on a low table beside the settee.

The silence was suddenly awkward. Is he really here, Andrea asked herself, as she sipped coffee. It seemed too unreal, too dreamlike.

When the silence became too long and she could bear it no longer, she held out her hand and Gabriel took her empty cup. His fingertips brushed hers. They were cold, although she could hear the roar of the gas fire and feel its warmth on her legs.

'Jane,' she said abruptly, 'I can get myself to bed. Only . . . Gabby and I have so much to catch up with, and . . . '

'Oh, sure thing.' Andrea heard the rattle of cup and saucer and a thump as they landed on the table. 'I'll hit the sack then.'

'Night Jane,' called Andrea and Gabriel in unison, and Andrea hoped Jane wasn't aware of the relief she felt.

Jane's departure left embarrassed swirls of deep silence. Only the swish of tyres on a wet road ebbed and flowed like the ocean.

'Andy. I don't know where to begin.' He clutched her fingers until she flinched.

'Sorry.' He loosened his grip and ran his thumb up and down the back of her hand.

Gradually her body relaxed with the rhythm of the cars, his caressing finger, the enclosed room, the hiss and pop of the gas fire, the sense of unreality.

'You're not wearing a ring Andy.'

Puzzled, she shook her head.

He cleared his throat. 'I thought you and Simon would be married by now. He said at the hospital that . . . '

Her throat tightened. 'You were at the hospital?'

'Of course.' His voice was strained. 'I returned from Germany as soon as I got news of Jennifer's . . . death. I went straight to the hospital to see you. Simon said you had broken bones, cuts and grazes but were otherwise in good shape. And that you had concussion and couldn't see anyone. He told me you were planning to marry . . . ' He paused. 'I wrote you a note and left.'

Her voice was thick with emotion. 'What did you say in the note Gabby?'

She heard his shaky indrawn breath. 'That I'd brought you nothing but bad luck and would bother you no more. I had wanted so much for you, and failed you, now I wouldn't stay around and mess it up for you. I wished you both . . . all the happiness in the world.'

They remained silent, each wrapped up in the vivid pictures they retained in their memories.

'I didn't get your note,' she said at last. 'I wouldn't have been able to see it anyway.'

'I wasn't told about . . . your sight Andy.'

Quickly she replied, 'I wanted no one told. Especially the public. I wanted no pity.'

'It must have been such a distressing time Andy.' His arm fell across her shoulders, resting there lightly.

'I wasn't aware of much for the first few weeks,' she admitted. 'The pain started when I recovered from the concussion unable to see or walk.' Her voice hardened. 'In those circumstances you struggle for survival, everything goes into keeping a grip on yourself, emotionally and physically. I remembered nothing about the accident.

'No,' she finished, 'I didn't think of much, apart from getting through each day, quite honestly.'

'I understand,' he said quietly. Then, 'You must have hated me.'

'Oh no,' she cried. 'Your wife was responsible for the fire. You were right, she was sick. Simon told me nothing about her death. It wasn't until much later that the doctor told me. I had no idea of your whereabouts. I read no papers, you see.'

'I went to the States,' he explained.

'And I, to my parents in Australia.'

'I asked about you,' he admitted, 'whenever I was on the phone to England. But you'd disappeared from

196

the face of the earth. I assumed you and Simon had made a new life somewhere, together.'

'How strange it all was,' she murmured.

'Andrea, what happened that night? Why were you there? I couldn't understand . . . '

She told him what had happened, from the time she received the note until she dragged his wife from the bedroom. For the first time since the accident, she recalled it all vividly. He pulled her to him until her head rested upon his shoulder and she felt his breath on her hair as he bent to listen.

'What do you mean, you heard me on the phone in the bedroom?' he questioned.

'I found her in the room with a cassette player. It was a tape I heard Gabby.'

'I see,' he said heavily. 'When I was away from home I sometimes sent her tapes instead of letters — just chatting about the show — everyday things — you know.'

Andrea nodded. Her heart pounded as she recalled that day. 'I tried to drag her out; she refused to come. I smelled drink Gabby.' Her voice broke. 'The last I remember is trying to force her down the stairs away from the fire . . . ' She shuddered.

His arm about her tightened. 'You ran into the house to save me Andy?' His voice was husky, and she raised a hand to touch his face, tracing with wonder the tear-filled grooves she had loved so much.

'What happened Gabby? Why did she do it?'

He sighed. 'Don had been treating her for depression for a number of years. You remember Don?'

Andrea shook her head. 'I never kept the appointment Gabby.'

'Oh. Well, there were a number of things he pointed to. Rejected by her mother — longing for a child of her own. When she lost our baby, the shock hit her more badly than it might otherwise have done.'

Beneath Andrea's searching fingers his throat constricted. 'Don felt that Jennifer married solely to have a home and a baby of her own. When she knew she couldn't have another child, there was no longer any need to be a wife. Yet she was terrified of loneliness.'

He shrugged. 'Who can say exactly what goes on in a person's mind. She was a bitter, lonely woman. And towards the end unstable enough to require hospital treatment. I knew she was dangerous Andrea. That's why I had to keep her from finding out about you. I should never have left her alone, but I had the band to think about and somehow, after I lost you, I felt iced up inside. I no longer always allowed Jennifer to interfere with my movements quite so much. I told her that if she couldn't cope on her own she could return to the nursing home.' He sighed. 'Once again I made an error of judgement.'

'No Gabby, no. We can't be so responsible for another person.'

His fingers pressed her shoulder. 'After the accident Don said that panic in the face of loneliness can drive such a woman into doing terrible things.'

'Poor woman,' Andrea said softly. 'And poor Gabby. You tried so hard.'

'What happened between you and Simon?' he asked.

'He was full of plans . . . until the doctor told him my blindness would be permanent. He left.'

Gabriel's fingers dug into her shoulder. 'Andy. You were so alone and you lost so much. Your sight, the singing you loved, your fiancé.'

She gave a harsh laugh. 'I never accepted Simon's proposal. After the accident he met a young boy singer whom he felt he could make into a star. That's what he wanted. Not a woman to love, but a star.'

'So you went to Australia,' he pressed.

She nodded. 'For two years. Didn't work out though. My parents tried, but

Dad couldn't cope well with a blind and crippled daughter.'

Restlessly she twisted in his arms. 'They fussed too much, and I really believe Dad was embarrassed to be seen with me.'

'Andrea!'

'I understand Gabby. I didn't blame them. Australia is a country for the fit and healthy. Besides,' she grinned, 'I didn't like flying cockroaches in my salad, or plagues of mice, not to mention spiders and snakes. Not being able to see, it was awful when someone suddenly shouted 'Andrea! don't move'.' She shuddered.

Gabriel laughed. 'Did you meet Jane there?'

'Yes. Her father had married again and she didn't get on with her stepmother. She's a funny girl, abrasive, self-contained, quiet. People don't warm to her. But we hit it off right away and she has a caustic sense of humour; a wicked way of describing people we meet which has me in hysterics at times. Looking after her father for so long she's good at running a home. She wanted to see England — I needed a companion; it's worked beautifully. She treats me as an equal, doesn't fuss too much. Although she's fairly protective.'

'I've noticed.'

They laughed together then, laughter that pushed away the skulking shadows. Until Andrea's laugh died, her eyes widened and darkened. He saw the dawn of reality there. For the past hour she had lived in the past, seeing life as it was. Memories had pushed away darkness as their laughter had disturbed the shadows. He saw the struggle in her eyes and understood. She was trying desperately to pierce the darkness; to see him again.

'Don't Andy.' His voice was soft. 'Don't darling.'

Gently he kissed each eyelid, holding her to him, catching her salty tears with his loving mouth. So that when his lips finally met hers, she tasted her own tears.

14

'Stothert & Son.'

'Andrea?'

'Hello Gabriel.'

'Darling, can I meet you from work tonight, I have something very exciting to tell you?'

'Well . . . all right. I finish at five. I'll phone Jane's office and ask her to go straight home instead of meeting me here.'

'See you then,' he said cheerfully.

She was sitting in the reception area when he walked in. He watched her for a while, wondering at the stillness which made her so unlike the girl he had known. She had indeed become a beautiful woman, he thought. The longer fashions gave her an elegant air, and her thinness an ethereal, model-girl quality. In splendid and intriguing contrast were the rounded cheek-bones she had so hated, and the small mouth. Today she had pinned her hair up on to her head, making her neck look long, especially as she had a habit of looking upwards, chin raised in the air. He noticed she rarely looked down.

Always upwards.

The expression on her face was touching, as she thought herself to be unobserved. It had a patience, which, although sweet, disturbed him. He had known her as a fighter. But then, she'd had her share of fighting, and he all at once felt intrusive standing there observing her without her knowledge.

His shoes squeaked when he crossed the parquet floor, and she turned her head, recognition lighting her face before he spoke. She rose, wearing flat-heeled shoes, and he towered above her.

He led her out of the building into the city street. 'We'll get a cab.'

She heard the squeal of brakes. 'You're doing it again,' she warned, settling into the leather seat.

'What?' He slid in beside her and slammed the door.

'Kidnapping me,' she laughed. 'I hope you have good reason.'

'I have.' His voice sounded triumphant, and she felt excitement, like waves of electricity, flowing from his body.

The taxi stopped and started; from outside came the roar of cars and buses as the city went home and commerce closed its doors.

'Why did you do it Gabby?'

'Do what darling?'

'Kidnap me. Be so persistent. Five years ago, I mean.'

He sighed. 'I fell in love with a voice.'

She tensed, waiting to hear him continue with words of love. Yet he said nothing, and her throat thickened with disappointment. What is it, she fretted, that causes a barrier between us. He's warm, loving and concerned, yet at the same time remote.

'Where are we going Gabby?' she asked in a small voice.

'You'll see.' Then he caught his breath.

'Don't,' she said swiftly. 'Don't be self-conscious about it and watch everything you say.'

The taxi turned, and the roar of traffic died to a faint hum. They were in a side road, she guessed, as the taxi crawled. And a smelly one, she realized, sniffing. The taxi stopped, Gabriel helped her out. She wrinkled her nose. Rotting food and dustbins.

'Up one step,' he whispered in her ear.

Obediently she lifted her foot. The step was uneven and dipped in the middle.

'Which theatre are we in?' she asked, tight lipped.

'The Royal.' He manoeuvred her along the passage and she breathed in the scent she would never forget. There was an air of peace; their footsteps rang loudly on the stone floor. But like flies, memories buzzed all around — rushing chorus girls, stale scent, dusty and steamy dressing-rooms, peeling paint, grimy windows, the lights around the mirror. A harassed Harold with his enormous kind eyes.

She heard Gabriel's knuckles meet wood. A hoarse voice called out. 'Come in.'

'Andrea.' Arms, warm and flabby. Cigar scent. A wet kiss landing on both cheeks. The brush of whiskers. 'Andrea, my dear. I'm so glad to see you.'

'Harold.' It was all she could say for the lump in her throat.

Gabriel led her to a settee. 'What have you done?' she whispered, perching uncomfortably on hard springs.

'I had the surprise of my life darling when I bumped into Gabriel and he said he'd met you again.' Harold's voice trembled and he sounded breathless. 'We've so often wondered . . . '

Andrea listened, with eyes narrowed, suspiciously trying on the tone of his voice. She felt on tenterhooks, anxious not to hear pity and prepared to feel anger if she did. She prodded every inflection in their voices, testing them out, because she felt stripped bare and — cowering in the corner of the settee — wounded.

Gabriel's hand pressed hers. 'Relax darling. You're among friends. Stop looking so hurt.'

'You were cruel to bring me here,' she burst out.

She heard the clink of glass and felt the coldness of a tumbler between her hands. She recognized the softness of Harold's touch as he supported her fingers until the glass was safe.

The smile sounded in his voice, she imagined the grin split from ear to ear. 'Just a drop of whisky and soda, to celebrate.'

'Celebrate what?' she snapped.

'Why . . . finding you, of course.'

Andrea sensed warning glances passing between them; felt like a child being placated. She wanted to scream, 'Look I'm blind, not stupid. Nor am I a child. I didn't lose my years or my brain with my sight, you stupid fools.' Instead, she flung Harold's hand away and took a gulp of the burning liquid, feeling it straight away anaesthetize the ache in her throat.

'And now you've found me, just what do you intend to do with me?'

Again the silence.

Harold cleared his throat.

But it was Gabriel who asked her. 'How would you like to come back Andrea?'

Gritting her teeth she raised her sightless eyes to the ceiling.

Gabriel started again. 'Andy. Harold and I were reminiscing about your lovely voice and what a waste it is that no one can hear it.'

A chair scraped the floor — Harold moved closer to the settee. 'I have, unfortunately, no space in this show darling, but I know someone who has.'

'So?' Her fingers played with a button on her coat.

'At the Lowminster Playhouse.'

Andrea frowned. 'Where's that?'

'A new town.' Harold's words started

to fall over themselves. 'Twinned with a French town. The Playhouse has chosen for its first revue a French theme. Perfect for your voice Andrea. There will be the usual things — can-can girls, men in berets . . . '

A tremulous smile forced Andrea's lips apart. 'Strings of onions.'

At once she felt the tension ease.

'I promise that you won't have to wear onions,' chortled Harold.

'Or plastic macs,' she added, on a wave of nostalgia.

'What are you two on about,' laughed Gabriel.

'Private joke,' she smiled. 'But Harold, how can I possibly, like this?'

'You'll get the job darling. Because once Bernard hears your voice he'll want no one else.'

She fought back rising excitement. 'Is it possible?'

Gabriel's voice, quiet and firm. 'Believe us Andy.'

★ ★ ★

'So this is Andrea.' Bernard pumped her hand up and down. 'My kids used to go to all your performances.'

Andrea smiled politely, trying to get a mental picture of the man, and of her surroundings. They sat in an office. The air outside the theatre had smelled clean and fresh, reminding her of her childhood. The theatre itself, as they walked through it to get to the office, had smelled more like a school, she thought. Antiseptic, chalky, a hint of coffee.

She was puzzled by her lack of nerves at the audition. Perhaps she never quite believed she would be chosen, it seemed such an impossible dream. Perhaps her darkness held her away from reality and made it easier to forget those watching. It wasn't a perfect performance, far from it. She missed her cue at the beginning and the pianist went off without her. But after five years that was to be expected, Bernard assured her.

By the time she had sung two

numbers she felt her confidence returning, and when Jane led her off-stage it
was to be told by Bernard that he
would like her to attend the first
rehearsal in ten days' time.

'Imagine it Andrea. The backcloth
— a picture of the Eiffel Tower.
You standing on the bridge over the
Seine. Jane can help you on to
the bridge before the curtain goes
up. You lean against it, and sing.
Simple.'

Gabriel added, 'Another scene takes
place in Montmartre. The backcloth
will have a picture of the Sacré Coeur
church. You'll stand on the balcony
singing to the people below. The poor
people of Paris.'

Despite herself Andrea started to
tingle. 'It might work.'

Jane sniffed. 'What about your job
Andy?'

'I'll hand in my notice.'

Sensing Jane's unspoken question,
she rushed on, 'I'll need your help,
Jane.'

Bernard answered for her. 'Jane comes too.'

In the car going home Andrea chatted excitedly. Jane sat silently on the back seat.

'Unfortunately, by the time your show starts I'll be at the Hippodrome,' said Gabriel.

'Oh Gabby.'

'I don't like missing your first night, but that's show business. And . . . you have what you want Andy.'

She was silent.

'You'll be a success. I know it,' he went on. 'Once you get your confidence back and become known, you'll start cutting discs. Your sight won't matter in a recording studio Andy.'

'It's the audience, Gabby. I know I can't see them now, but I shall feel them. I like an audience. Making records never appealed to me.'

He continued as if she hadn't spoken, 'There will be nothing to stand in your way Andrea. Right Jane?'

'Don't ask me! I'd not heard Andrea

sing until that time at the firm's dinner.'

Gabriel, as always, seemed able to read Andrea's thoughts. 'Don't go getting yourself into a panic Andy. Remember that nothing has changed really. Your voice is the same, possibly even better with maturity. Your limp is scarcely noticeable. You were a hit five years ago, and can be again.'

'Fame itself is frightening Gabby.'

'It's what you want though.'

'I know. You start off aiming for it, yet really it's a dream — a sort of it-will-never-happen-to-me feeling. Then it happens, and you're never ever ready.'

She turned her head towards the back seat. 'I never told you much about those days did I Jane?'

'No.'

'I realize now, why I had such awful moods. It was because I was unready for the change brought about by fame. The only stable thing in my life was Gabriel.'

'Oh, Andy . . . '

'Don't start blaming yourself Gabby.

I clung to you because I could find no other firm ground to stand upon. The world changes with fame; it's a very lost feeling. One has to be mature enough to take it. I wasn't.'

'I didn't realize,' said Jane slowly. 'I knew you once sang a bit, but I had no idea you were such a star.'

Andrea laughed. 'I almost was, wasn't I Gabby?'

'To me you always were darling.'

Her heart missed a beat. What did he mean? Was it his way of saying I love you, or just theatrical drama?

'Did you ever think of re-marrying Gabriel?' she asked, holding her breath.

'Yes. Of course. I no longer have any need to live like a monk, Andy. Now come on you two, out you get, it's getting late. Sweet dreams.'

She was older and wiser, too sensible now to have her emotions knocked about by that man, Andrea reminded herself as Jane struggled with door keys. No longer was she subject to the emotional mood swings of her youth.

Yet . . . being with Gabriel Fox was still like walking on shifting sands.

Damn him.

15

'The dress is black, with scooped neckline and floor-length full skirt,' announced Jane.

Andrea smiled to herself. 'You don't like it?'

'It's so plain,' Jane groaned.

'I'm supposed to look elegant,' Andrea remonstrated.

Jane's voice was muffled. Andrea heard the creak of cane. 'There are long black gloves and a scarf.'

'A breeze will be blowing while I stand on the bridge,' explained Andrea. 'Just enough to float the scarf and move my hair a little. To add realism.'

'Very clever,' Jane drawled.

Andrea sighed. If only they could share the excitement together. She had expected Jane to be interested in what went on behind the scenes in a theatre, albeit a provincial one, but the girl didn't seem to fit. She was brusque with the lovable, if irascible, people they worked with, horrified at their familiarity, their hugs, kisses and endearments. And she had developed a clumsy trait which Andrea hadn't noticed before.

Then her heart smote her. The poor girl was in a strange environment. She had spent her youth in the outback and her teens caring for her father. Who could blame her for feeling like a fish out of water in the maelstrom of theatreland? Where is my understanding, Andrea scolded herself?

'What have you found?' She reached out a hand, seeking contact and found Jane's bony shoulder.

'Nothing much. A scruffy red dress.'

'For the balcony scene,' Andrea guessed. 'I'm supposed to be very poor. There should be a shawl too.'

'There is. I'd better hang these things up, the room's a mess.'

'Thanks Jane. I won't need them until dress rehearsal tomorrow.' She felt a tremor of delight. Dress rehearsal.

Then the opening.

Her thoughts flew to Gabriel, and her excitement died. Only two telephone calls in three weeks.

The wardrobe door creaked, hangers rattled.

There was a crash. 'Bloody thing,' muttered Jane to the object that had tripped her up.

Probably the wicker basket which took up most of the tiny room. Andrea sighed. What was the matter with the girl? Always so cross lately. It had been a relief to talk to Gabriel the day before yesterday. To be talking to someone who understood, who sympathized with her doubts and fears, shared her excitement.

Andrea's face grew warm. She had come very near to asking Gabriel why he hadn't been to see her on Sunday. If only she could hear him say he would be coming. What was the matter with all of them? She blinked away tears. This was her big chance.

There again was the strange yearning

she remembered from five years ago. The need to be by his side. The need that had swept her along to seek him out at Tanglewood that fateful Sunday. Probably his wife had seen them together, Andrea admitted to herself, remembering the shadow at the window which might not have been the sun's reflection. If she hadn't chased him like that . . . he wouldn't have confessed he loved her . . .

Andrea jumped up. 'Jane. Will you dial Gabriel's telephone number for me?'

She stood in a whirlwind of activity, hugging the wall and clinging to the receiver, hardly able to hear his voice above the hubbub in the corridor.

Throwing away caution she told him she had missed him. 'I was just thinking about you,' she finished.

'Didn't want to pressurize you darling, you know what a beast I can be when I'm driving you. In any case I have a friend here from the States, and she's kept me busy. You know what

Americans are — I've had to show her all the sights, well some of them, in between doing the show.'

Andrea swallowed. 'I see.'

'On stage,' came the call.

'I have to go,' she muttered.

'I know, I heard it. Good luck darling.'

'Right Jane,' she called, fighting the lump in her throat, 'Let's go.'

The corridors echoed with pounding feet and excited voices.

'Careful,' warned Jane. 'There are paint pots and things everywhere — scenery sailing about — so many people! Mind the trailing wires.'

Andrea smelled sickly paint fumes and the fresh scent of wood. Heard the rasp of saws and chorus of hammers. Lighting technicians snapped commands, scenery squeaked and rattled its way across the floor; machinery whirred. Bernard, she knew, would be somewhere out front, and if he was anything like Harold, running fingers through his hair until it stood on end.

She hoped for his sake that by the time the curtain rose all would be a little calmer on the seething stage.

★　★　★

It was the following day. The black skirt swirled around her legs. Jane placed her in the centre of the bridge and arranged the dress. Andrea rested her hands lightly on the parapet. Thank goodness, she thought, this is only dress rehearsal. She wasn't ready to stand alone. Would she ever be? The fearsome question grabbed her around the throat and drenched her body with fear; her weak leg ached. Taking all her weight on her good leg she leaned against the parapet.

Suddenly there was nothing in her hands — she was grasping at air.

'Look out,' someone yelled. 'The bridge . . . '

There was a crash. She had a frightful sense of teetering on the edge of the world. But Jane's hands were around her waist, pulling her backwards and leading her off stage.

'I told you it was a foolish idea,' Jane yelled. 'I knew it wasn't safe.'

Denials and exclamations bounded around the stage from the props men and stage hands. Savagely disappointed Andrea shook herself free from Jane's arm, trying not to show how she was trembling.

'We'll rehearse without the bridge,' roared Bernard, 'and hope you can get the thing repaired by tonight.'

Andrea flinched for the carpenters. She felt Bernard's hot breath on her face and the dampness of his hand. 'Are you OK, Andrea?'

She nodded, her heart beating fast. 'I'll do the song now. Get me a chair.'

He patted her shoulder. 'Good girl.' And walked off muttering.

'You look ill, Andy,' said Jane. 'You're very pale.'

Andrea's mouth was dry with fear. 'I'm perfectly all right. Just superstition.'

'Superstition?'

'An accident at dress rehearsal is a bad omen.'

'You don't have to go on with it.'

Shocked, Andrea limped through the curtains to reach the stage. 'I do. Oh yes I do. You don't understand show business Jane,' she snapped.

'If I hadn't been there you'd have fallen,' Jane retorted.

Without replying Andrea limped on stage, welcomed by the opening bars of her song, and resting against a chair-back, simply stood and sang.

★   ★   ★

As the last note of her balcony song died away, Andrea felt Jane's arm go lightly around her waist. She pressed her friend's hand. 'Thanks Janie.'

Despite the earlier accident the rest of rehearsal had gone well, and she was exuberant as Jane helped her down the steps behind the curtain.

She felt for each step with care, sliding one hand down the rail and clutching Jane's hand with the other.

'Telephone Andrea,' called the Stage Manager. He helped her down the last step and kissed her cheek. 'Well done darling.'

'Thanks Roy.' Hugging the receiver to her ear, she tried to cut out the surrounding noise.

'How did the dress rehearsal go?' asked Gabriel.

'There was an accident this afternoon.' She recounted the story of the bridge.

He laughed. 'You're not superstitious, are you?'

'Not until something happens. The same as all of us.' Her voice trembled. 'I feel so much better for talking to you.'

'Mind your back luv.' She squeezed herself into the wall as two men forced their way past her, dragging something heavy along the ground.

'I didn't hear you,' she called anxiously into the telephone.

'I said — would you like me to be there tonight?'

'Can you? What about the show, and your . . . friend?'

'I'll fix it darling. I'll bring Charlotte with me.'

The phone went down.

With a thumping heart she replaced the receiver and leaned against the wall. 'He's coming to the show tonight Jane. Thank God.'

'I see.' Jane sounded distracted.

In the dressing-room Andrea tried to relax on the settee while Jane plugged in the electric kettle and opened a jar of instant coffee.

'You're in love with Gabriel, aren't you Andrea?'

Andrea felt warmth spread through her body. 'Yes. Yes, I am. But he's a strange guy Jane.'

'What do you mean?'

Andrea heard the sizzle of boiling water on granules, the clink of a spoon. Jane always stirred drinks as if she was beating eggs.

'He can be so old-fashioned,' she began. 'So cautious, I could shake him.

He's oblivious to hints or suggestions.' She bit her lip, adding quickly. 'I admit I was a bit forward once; I was young, attracted to him, and let him know it. He merely treated me like a child.'

'He was married, though, wasn't he?'

'Ye-s. I know what you're thinking; I'm not proud of myself for chasing a married man. But his marriage was on the rocks when I came along. Besides, I wasn't sure that he was married at first, gossip said he wasn't.'

'When you found out, though, you would have gone with him by the sound of it.'

'He asked me to,' Andrea retorted. 'But I refused.'

'He asked you to marry him?'

'No. He asked me to have an affair with him.' Andrea's voice was grave as all the hurt of that time rushed back. 'He said he could never leave his wife.'

'Just like a man,' came the brusque reply. 'Totally dishonest.'

'That's very cynical Jane,' Andrea

began, then stopped, remembering how she had seen Gabriel's sacrifice in just that way, not believing in a love that puts the other person first.

'In that case,' said Jane triumphantly, 'Gabriel's free now. Has he asked you to marry him?'

'No,' Andrea admitted in a low voice. She took a gulp of coffee. 'I'm sure he cares about me, he shows it often. Then he seems to hold back. I don't know what he's afraid of. There's this girl, Charlotte, he's never mentioned her before . . . Jane, do you . . . do you think it's anything to do with me? My blindness, I mean?'

'It could be, love. You should face up to that possibility. Many men would be — well — put off.'

'Perhaps his concern has been out of the guilt he seems to feel, and . . . pity,' Andrea sighed.

There was the crash of cups and water spurted into the handbasin. 'Perhaps,' called Jane, 'he realized you're taking his concern for something

more and he's staying away on pur-
pose.'

Andrea jumped up from the settee.
'I'm too restless to sit still. Will you take
me for a walk Jane, there isn't time to
go home and I need some air?'

The roller towel rasped. 'You'll sure
get that Andrea. You can keep your
English seaside towns in summer. But if
that's what you want . . . '

'Bless you Jane. What would I do
without you?'

'You don't have to. Here, wear a
jacket.'

* * *

Jane held the door open for Andrea to
re-enter the dressing-room. 'Your hair is
all over the place, it will need doing.
What a wind!'

Andrea paused. She could smell
sandalwood. 'It's good to have you here
Gabby,' she said politely.

His hands were gentle on her
shoulders. 'I couldn't stay away.'

'Stop trying,' she snapped.

In the silence her heart thumped madly. Had her usual awkwardness spoilt a magic moment? 'Is Charlotte here?'

'She's out front.' His voice was non-committal, Andrea could read nothing into it at all.

Jane's strident voice startled her. 'Time to dress.' From the corridor came a deep singsong voice. 'Beginners please.'

Andrea felt Gabriel move away. 'I'm delaying you. Off you go and dress. Remember that audience of yours. I know you can't see them now, but they're in your memory. Up to row J. Good luck darling.'

She felt his lips on her hair. The door closed.

Jane led her to the dressing-table. She sat on the stool and reached out, feeling the heat of the lights around the mirror. 'Help me with my make-up Jane.'

★   ★   ★

230

Through draughty corridors — smell of greasepaint, gin and fear. Artificial laughter. High heels clattering on an iron staircase — strains of music.

'Good luck Andrea.'

'Thanks Roy.'

'Let me take your coat Andrea. Good luck.'

'Up the stairs you go darling. Careful.'

The cold rail beneath her hand, her feet groping for each step. The red dress clinging around her knees as she climbed — Jane's footsteps clanging behind.

'You're there,' called Jane, reaching past Andrea to part the heavy drapes.

Andrea stepped on to the tiny balcony. Jane was beside her, arranging the shawl, fussing with the dress. Straightening, pulling, tugging.

From below came the voices of the chorus.

'I'll be right behind you, out of sight,' Jane whispered, kissing her cheek. Andrea was startled. Both at the sign of affection and the smell of gin. She hadn't realized Jane drank gin. But it ran so freely here . . .

Moths whisked around her stomach, and in sudden terror, she gripped the front of the balcony. The chorus was reaching the end of the overture; the curtain would be rising to expose the balcony where she stood. The spotlight would be on her.

Gabby was out there. He was her audience. There would be the spotlight, her pathway to the stars, glittering with particles of dust. Suddenly it was there, lighting her darkness, the point when she knew it was hopeless. She had no voice. She wouldn't be able to sing. But she opened her mouth anyway.

The notes floated out, a little shaky at first, but with every one her confidence grew, and she forgot the chorus below, singing instead to the audience. The fidgety, the still, the lovers, windswept holiday-makers, tired landladies and shop assistants, the bored, the worried, and Gabriel. Breathing deeply she let the warm, low notes slide down each breath to land true and strong at the feet of the people.

Applause came as no surprise, dripping like a transfusion into her veins. Oh, I've missed this — I've missed it so, she cried to herself.

Burning with emotion she leaned forward, reaching out to the people who were loving her. She sensed the heavy curtain dropping — the applause became muted.

The balcony front leapt from her hands. She heard a crash and screams. Terrifying space sucked her down like a stone into a pit. Her hands clawed through air. There was a sickening thump and excruciating pain in the back of her head. The roar of applause echoed and rebounded as if she lay in the bottom of a well. Ebbing and flowing like ocean waves. And leaping in and out of the waves — pain. Darting like fishes in a dark sea.

A much darker darkness than before.

16

Balls of light . . . floating around her face . . . like puffs of cotton wool . . .

I must be in my dressing-room, she thought, before everything went black.

She awoke in a room smelling of antiseptic. She was high up — not far below the white plastic lampshade. Light splashed on to a white coverlet, the ceiling was in shadow, the walls could have been white or yellow, the floor was a pool of deep shining blue. The door had a porthole.

On her head she wore a very tight hat and crossly she raised her hand to take it off.

'Andy. You're awake.'

She turned her head towards the voice and pain flashed like lightning across her eyes. A face rose from below — a face creased and with red-rimmed eyes.

She touched his hair. 'There's silver among the black now Gabby.'

The bed bounced. He was beside her. She winced, conscious that her body ached all over. He swallowed.

And his eyes seemed to pierce her soul.

When she would have tried again to remove the hat he grasped her hand with an urgent, panicky movement.

'You can see me Andy?' he demanded.

'Yes.' She struggled to sit up, gasping when pain shot through her head and eyes. 'I can. I can.' She began to tremble from head to toe.

'Hey. Stay still. We don't know what . . . '

'Please Gabby. What happened?'

'There was an accident — you fell from the balcony.'

Her head fell back on the pillow, her eyes roamed the room. 'Gabby.' She sat up. 'Please. Lift me up. Take me to the mirror.' She pointed to the mirror over a handbasin in the corner of the room.

He glanced at the door. 'Nurse popped out for a minute. I must tell her you've come round.'

'Please Gabby.'

'Darling, there's . . . ' His voice went gruff.

'What is it?' she asked quickly, raising her hand to her face.

'It's just that your head is bandaged . . . '

'Is that all. For a moment . . . ' Andrea's heart thumped. 'Please Gabby. Never mind the bandages.'

Reluctantly he pulled back the bed clothes and she felt the hardness of his arms as he carried her across the room. In the dim light a stranger stared back at her.

Against her face, nearly as white as the bandage, her eyes were dark and sombre, shadowed with blue smudges. It was the expression of wariness and resignation there that had altered. And her forehead was exposed, making her face less round.

'That's not me.'

'It is. The woman you've become. A beautiful lady.'

She struggled to accept herself, when all the time she had imagined herself as she used to be. Her hand stretched out towards the mirror. 'No lights.'

He carried her back across the room, lowering her on to the bed and tucking the sheet and coverlet around her. 'You'll have all the lights you want Andy. The audience loved you. I'll call the nurse now.'

Pain swept across her brow and she closed her eyes, trembling with fear. He had retreated from her, she sensed it. Why? Something to do with the theatre . . .

The nurse bustled in, followed by the doctor. 'Wait outside, Mr Fox.'

Andrea opened her eyes. 'Don't go Gabby.'

'Shush,' warned the doctor. 'Let me look at you.'

Andrea tried to relax, feeling as if the cool fingers and torch probed down to her feet.

'Mm. You must lie quietly with no lights and with the blind drawn for the next few hours. I know you must be aching to fling yourself out into the world to stare; I understand completely how you feel.' His large brown eyes reminded her of Harold. 'But we don't know yet . . . ' he pursed his lips.

Andrea tensed, sick with fear. 'You think my sight might go again Doctor?'

He shook his head. 'Your case isn't unusual. There have been other cases of sight returning after a blow. But not always, you understand, one hundred percent. Sometimes the sight is impaired, sometimes as good as new; and again, sometimes the sight returns in one eye only.'

She took a deep breath and tried to calm her thumping heart. 'Well . . . '

He smiled tightly. 'We must take it easy my dear. See what happens.'

Disturbed by the doctor's gentle warning, she was lying with eyes closed, terrified to move, when she heard the door click.

She opened her eyes. A basket exploding with colour appeared to be flying towards her with Gabriel's face hovering behind.

'You spoke to the doctor?' she asked anxiously.

He placed the basket of flowers on the table and sat beside her on the bed.

'He seems only fifty percent certain I'll keep my sight,' she pressed.

'That's more hope than you had a week ago.' He reached for her hand. 'The flowers are from the theatre, by the way. They all send their love.'

She nodded. 'Thank them for me.'

'Sure. I phoned Harold, told him the news. He was in a state — you know Harold! I suspect you would rather tell your parents yourself.'

She nodded. 'Mustn't raise their hopes, in case . . . '

'You'll be fine. I know it.'

'What did Jane say?' she asked. 'Is she coming?'

In the heavy silence that followed, she saw his face cloud over, turning surly like the Gabby she remembered.

'Jane was hurt too?' she cried.

'You'll have to know some time darling.'

'Know what?'

'I'll start at the beginning.'

'I wish you would. I hate mysteries.'

'The dress rehearsal,' he began heavily, 'when the bridge broke. Darling — Jane unbolted the front section.'

'That's silly,' Andrea said stoutly.

He gripped her fingers tightly. 'And when she helped you on to the balcony, I suppose she knelt down and fussed around your dress?'

'I don't . . . remember.'

'While she was doing so, she unbolted the front of the balcony. It was easy. You couldn't see, and you couldn't hear because the chorus on stage was singing.'

Sickened, she fought to understand his words. 'What are you trying to tell me? Jane's been a wonderful friend. The only woman friend I've ever had.'

Gabriel's voice was husky. 'I know

darling. But you see . . . I had a feeling, an instinct about it. She really thought, we all did, that you were more badly hurt than you are. It wasn't a high drop, but the way your head hit the ground . . . ' He shuddered. 'There was a look on her face . . . in the panic I thought no more of it, but afterwards it came back to me, niggled at me. When I returned from the hospital briefly last night, I exaggerated rather.' He gave a rueful smile. 'I let her think you . . . well, that you could die. I also said I was going to call in the police, that I was suspicious of the circumstances. She went off her head. Confessed to everything. At first she said it was a joke . . . '

Andrea gasped. 'A joke?'

'She begged me to tell you she was sorry and hadn't meant you any harm. She planned to catch you before you fell; she hadn't expected you to lean over the balcony the way you did. When you lay unconscious, she panicked, and I think it was then I saw something in her face, something that spoke of guilt.'

'Why, Gabby?' she whispered.

'She said show business was wrong for you; she wanted to show you, and probably Bernard, that it wouldn't work. Put you off the idea of returning to the stage. But I think it was jealousy.'

'Jealousy? Was she in love with you? Was it you she wanted?'

He shook his head. 'Not me. You. You're the sister she never had. Her family. Your career was a threat. You were all right as you were, she kept saying.'

Andrea remembered Jane's background, the girl's loneliness. 'I'm beginning to understand. Without me she has no one.'

'Thank God your colour's coming back. Yes, she was needed by you, and it wasn't in her plans for you to be a star. She preferred you to be dependent upon her.'

'Poor Jane. I can never seem to keep a woman friend.' Her half smile was rueful.

'That reminds me,' Gabriel said. 'There was a telephone call from Jill. Remember Jill?'

Andrea nodded.

'She phoned to congratulate you on your return and I had to tell her about the accident. She will be coming to see you.'

Andrea put a hand to her aching head. 'That will be nice. But do you know what I keep thinking?'

'What's that darling?'

'It's a silly thing to think of, but I haven't even seen Jane. I'll never know what she looked like.'

'Did you know about her face?'

Andrea frowned.

'Her scars,' he went on.

'She said she had a skin complaint . . . '

'I tried to get through to her once, I thought it would help her to talk about it. I can't say I ever liked the girl but for your sake I wanted to be friends. However, she would only say she'd been burned as a child, at a barbecue.'

Andrea drew in her breath.

He hesitated, then went on quietly, 'It must have been an appalling accident.'

'I wish I'd known,' said Andrea. 'I would have understood her more. She pushed people away, wouldn't allow herself to make friends, and I used to persuade her to come with me to social functions. I was so determined not to shut myself up and brood, I didn't give a thought to the reason for her shyness.'

'So with you fêted and courted, and eventually married, she faced loneliness,' said Gabriel.

'Did you say married?' Andrea asked.

He leaned forward and wiped the tears from her cheeks with a gentle finger. 'I did.' His thick black brows came together. 'I know the theatre is more important to you at the moment — I wasn't going to do anything to spoil it for you, but now . . . ' he sighed. 'Perhaps I'm being selfish again, but I do love you so much. And I long to take care of you. Keep you safe from harm.'

'What about Charlotte?' she whispered.

'Charlotte is someone I met,' he replied. 'She's a dear girl.'

'What's she like?'

He raised his eyes to the ceiling. 'What a curious girl you are. She's . . . small and dark, roundish, a bundle of fun.'

'Oh Gabby, maybe you need fun. I can be such a pain in the neck at times.'

What is this sort of love, she was thinking, that is truly concerned and caring? I can't help it — but I want him to be happy at last. Even if it means — someone else.

His eyes looked bleak. 'Trying to get rid of me?'

She caught her breath. 'I think,' she said softly, 'that we're both going around in circles trying to do the best for each other. And in doing so have caused a hell of a lot of misunderstanding. Let's start at the beginning. You love me, right?'

'Guilty.'

'And I love you.'

At the look of relief on his face, she broke into a smile. 'I don't know why we've made everything so complicated then; it's all really quite simple.' She put a finger to his lips, tracing the lines that swept up to his eyes. They held, she saw, the glowing light she could never put a name to.

Exhaustion clamped down upon her suddenly, and she slumped against the pillows, but her eyes clung to his face. 'Yes, I want them, the lights and the applause. But more than that I want the light of love in your eyes Gabby — it's a wondrous sight for a woman to see on the man she loves.'

His eyes glowed. 'It will never go out,' he promised, and moving closer he kissed her gently first on one eyelid then on the other. Then laid his head down against her breast, as if he too was tired.

She looked down at his dear head lying so close to her lips; touched the crisp black waves and strands of silver with gentle fingers, and looked across the room at the mirror — not yet able to believe that she could truly see again, that once more the bulbs would glow for her, around the dressing-table mirror. If all goes well.

Behind his head, she crossed her fingers.

What she held in her arms was held in her heart and she was filled with an extraordinary tenderness and a gentle, warm maturity, because out of the fire of real love rises the earth mother.

'I love you,' she whispered. Knowing that whatever happened — the lovelight in his eyes would be there with her for the rest of their lives.

THE END

We do hope that you have enjoyed reading this large print book.

Did you know that all of our titles are available for purchase?

We publish a wide range of high quality large print books including:
Romances, Mysteries, Classics, General Fiction, Non Fiction and Westerns.

Special interest titles available in large print are:
The Little Oxford Dictionary Music Book, Song Book Hymn Book, Service Book

Also available from us courtesy of Oxford University Press:
Young Readers' Dictionary (large print edition) Young Readers' Thesaurus (large print edition)

For further information or a free brochure, please contact us at:
Ulverscroft Large Print Books Ltd., The Green, Bradgate Road, Anstey, Leicester, LE7 7FU, England. Tel: (00 44) **0116 236 4325 Fax:** (00 44) **0116 234 0205**